"I'M SORRY, BUT THIS IS NOT OKAY," KASIDY SAID.

She was talking to herself as much as to Kira and Yevir, her words gathering speed as they poured out. "I can't stay here if this is what it's going to be like. I'm a person with a *life,* I'm not some indirect religious figure in a cause, and if you think I'm going to let my child be involved in any part of this particular dilemma, think again. Ten thousand Bajorans dying so that my baby will be born into peace, so that he or she can be worshiped as some kind of spiritual embodiment, as some *thing?*"

Kas folded her arms tighter and then deliberately relaxed them, so tuned to the second life inside her that she almost reflexively protected it now. It wasn't a matter of choice, her current priorities didn't allow for choice; she couldn't have this madness in her life.

"I'll leave," she said calmly. "I'll get as far away from here as possible."

Before anyone could speak, a man's unfamiliar voice spilled out of an open com on Ro's desk, deep and clear and very fast.

"Security alert, the Jem'Hadar soldier has killed at least two people and is no longer in containment. Starfleet medical officer down, needs emergency transport to medical facilities. This is Commander Elias Vaughn, acknowle

For orders other than by individual consumers, Pocket Books grants a discount on the purchase of **10 or more** copies of single titles for special markets or premium use. For further details, please write to the Vice President of Special Markets, Pocket Books, 1230 Avenue of the Americas, 9th Floor, New York, NY 10020-1586.

For information on how individual consumers can place orders, please write to Mail Order Department, Simon & Schuster, Inc., 100 Front Street, Riverside, NJ 08075.

STAR TREK
DEEP SPACE NINE®

AVATAR

BOOK TWO OF TWO

S.D. Perry

Based upon STAR TREK®
created by Gene Roddenberry,
and STAR TREK: DEEP SPACE NINE
created by Rick Berman & Michael Piller

POCKET BOOKS
New York London Toronto Sydney Singapore B'hala

An *Original* Publication of POCKET BOOKS

POCKET BOOKS, a division of Simon & Schuster, Inc.
1230 Avenue of the Americas, New York, NY 10020

This book is published by Pocket Books, a division of Simon & Schuster, Inc., under exclusive license from Paramount Pictures.

ISBN: 0-7434-0051-8

First Pocket Books printing May 2001

10 9 8 7 6 5 4 3 2 1

Cover art by Cliff Nielsen
New logo design by Michael Okuda

Printed in the U.S.A.

For Steve, Dianne, and Gwen
For home

ACKNOWLEDGMENTS

Same as the last book, so if you read it there, you can skip this part:

This book wouldn't have been possible without the kindness, creative improvements, and/or information provided to me by . . .

Paula Block, at Paramount, for her tremendous support. Keith R. A. DeCandido and David Henderson, who helped compile the time line. Doctor Joelle Murray, for a few physics definitions that I *think* I understand (Joelle: you rock). Cliff Nielsen for his brilliant cover art, and Mike Okuda, for the new logo design (sharp, eh?). Jessica McGivney, for always believing. Also, Rob Simpson, who was there at the story's conception . . . and of course, my editor, Marco Palmieri, who is a creative force behind these books but tries to avoid taking credit.

On a more personal note, I need to thank Steve and Dianne Perry, Doctor Les Goldmann, and Myk Olsen, for their moral support . . . and to every brave writer of *Star Trek* technical journals, encyclopedias, chronologies, and companions—without you, I'd still be writing the outline.

One meets destiny often on the road taken to avoid it.

—French Proverb

PROLOGUE

Odo sat on the speck of rock in the great golden sea, on the barren island where he had last seen her face, watching the ocean glimmer and wave. There were times when he had to wonder if the loneliness of Odo was worth holding on to, gazing out across the living surface; it was forever, and even in chaos, it was beautiful.

But with the loneliness always came memories of his life, and they reaffirmed his purpose. He sat on the warm rock where she'd last stood, where she'd smiled in love as he'd descended into the Link. He remembered feeling himself expand across their ocean, his ocean, feeling exhaustion and despair become peace for those he reached, as **they** reached others. Feeling hope, and experiencing possibility. It was a good memory, its beautiful, idealistic imagery making him want to remember others—times of mirth and confusion, feelings of friendship, and

Nerys, always Nerys. He held on to his memories, sharing but never relinquishing them, keeping them as treasured proof that she had loved him.

Now he sat looking out at the beckoning sea because there were things to consider. When he was Odo instead of One with the Link, he could organize his thoughts the way he'd always organized them, to make them understandable in a linear way . . . and more simply but no less important, he had taken form to help keep track of time, which was very different within the Link. Events were unfolding, and it would serve him well to be watchful.

The Link had not been at peace since the war's end, its unrest growing as each member rejoined, bringing information of their defeat's continuing outcome. News of the Dominion's grand failure had sparked rebellious disturbances on some of its subject worlds; the Vorta had been instructed to use the Jem'Hadar to maintain the Dominion's cherished order. Odo had extended the thought that force was only one of many alternatives, but it was being roundly ignored.

He told himself that the Great Link was just beginning a period of transition, that hurrying through it was impossible, but some of their beliefs and practices—violence against their subjects, the continued mistrust of solids, desires for retaliation and fear of reprisal—were frustrating and upsetting. The Link could examine and accept information easily enough, but there was still great trouble understanding.

Behind Odo, a sound of liquid taking form. He glanced back and then looked out over his family again, steeling himself for whatever reason Laas had come. It was usually Laas, when the Link wanted to reach Odo as solid; it was as though they thought Laas's temporary stay on DS9 made Odo more receptive to him. Odo was, in fact, mostly indifferent; Laas wasn't going to convince him of anything.

"It's decided that the Vorta will take soldiers to abolish unrest," Laas said.

Odo nodded, sighing. It had never really been in question, but he would keep proposing peaceful options, even knowing that they might fail. That was certainly one reason there was still such resistance to his thoughts; many had already decided his interests made him unreliable, unstable, and refused to listen.

Laas stepped closer, his own opinion clear in his voice, toneless but somehow slightly sneering. "We still don't think that anything will come of your plan," he said.

Odo scowled, turning to look up at him. "You speak for the Link now, Laas?"

"Most of it." The changeling didn't back down, but Odo noted that he didn't presume any further, either. "They're willing to wait and see what happens . . . but they believe the Alpha Quadrant will strike, as soon as they see an opportunity. The treaty was our death warrant. Solids are incapable of changing their prejudices."

Odo had heard it before, and it never ceased to amaze him. "It's as if they forgot who started the war," he scoffed.

Laas was getting angry. "We didn't attempt genocide. We didn't try to murder them all with disease."

It was a point often argued within the Link, its form at times distorted by the discord. Odo shook his head, always disheartened that he had to explain it again.

But if I repeat it often enough . . . He hoped, he proposed and reasoned, and until his persistence bore fruit, it was the best he could do. They would eventually get tired of his arguments and their own fear, it was inevitable, and then some would try listening to reason. The Link was stubborn, and it was angry and hurt . . . but he didn't believe that it was incapable of change.

"We are not all alike, as fragments of the Link—do you judge the Link by my actions?" Odo asked. "The disease was the work of extremists, a very few among very many, and only then because the Link had aroused the very fears and prejudices you ascribe to them. Inciting wars among the Alpha powers, abduction, terrorism, invasion . . ."

Laas frowned, the pity on his face infinitely worse for Odo than his contempt. "They tried to destroy the Link, Odo. Your obsession with promoting them, it isn't right. *We* are One, and you are One."

"And 'we' were also part of the Hundred, Laas," Odo said. "The Founders sent us out to seek and discover, to find and learn, in the hope that we would bring knowledge back to them. I've come home knowing that the solids are neither inferior nor evil, they're just not like us. Peace is possible."

Urged by feeling, Odo got to his feet, facing Laas. "This is the knowledge I've brought home to the Great Link, that I was sent away for. Shouldn't I be permitted to show them how things really are?"

"Your 'knowledge' is being heard," Laas said, his pity turned to resignation, his voice heavy with it.

"That the solids deserve our respect. You introduce this to us when we've lost so much by their hands . . . but we still listen, because we are Linked with you. All of this the Link does for you, and still you plead for *them.*"

Odo turned away, looking up and away from Laas and the shimmering gold sea, looking into the sky. Laas stepped from the rock and was gone.

They would listen. They would learn.

Odo saw stars, pale in the dark and faraway, and thought of Nerys. He was concerned for her. She was the reason that he was here, she was how he knew that the Link was wrong, and she was out there now, dealing with what he'd set in motion. Events that might eventually provide evidence for his cause, for *their* cause—but that might also be hard on her. She was the strongest person he'd ever known, but he couldn't foresee all the possible consequences of his actions.

Odo sat down again, leaning back against a raised formation of rock so he could keep looking at the sky. He could only keep telling the truth; he would have to wait for news.

I

After Ro left, Kira sat down, staring at the book and its translation, feeling strangely numb. It was almost as though Reyla's murder had triggered a chain of miseries, as though the man who had killed her had introduced chaos and disaster to them all.

Within the last three days, Reyla's murder, then the Jem'Hadar attack. Now the Federation is coming, weapons ready, we've got a Jem'Hadar locked up who says that Odo sent him here on a mission of peace . . . and now this.

As unhappy and tired as she was, the thought almost made her smile, a giddy reaction to the unlikely summary of events. It sounded ludicrous, the details and circumstances only adding to the implausibility of it all.

Yes, and people have died.

The thought sobered her instantly. She picked up the translation, scrolling through a few pages. She opened the book's front cover again, looking at the strangely flowing symbols. No author's mark.

Ro's voice, the open worry on her face. *Colonel, I'm not prone to leaps of faith, you probably know that, but everything in that book has come true. Everything.*

Kira concentrated on the translation, moving back to the text that Ro had shown her, considering her security chief's credibility as the words skipped by. Whatever the difficulties between them, Ro had presented her findings clearly, her deductions sound: Istani Reyla had brought a book of Bajoran prophecy to the station and hidden it, perhaps because she knew that someone wanted to take it from her. The as yet unidentified killer had stabbed her for the bag she carried, and had almost certainly fallen to his death believing that he had the book. All of this suggested that the artifact was extremely important.

Kira wasn't sure about a lot of things when it came to her new security officer, but Ro's intelligence had never been in question. Nor had her reading skills.

Kira read the marked passage again; according to the padd, it was the last complete prophecy. Pages from before and after the text were gone, ripped from the book.

> *. . . with the Herald attendant. A New Age for Bajor will begin with the birth of the alien Avatar, an age of Awareness and Understanding beyond what the land's children have ever known. The child Avatar will be the second of the Emissary, he to whom the Teacher Prophets sing, and will be born to a gracious and loving*

world, a world ready to Unite. Before the birth, ten thousand of the land's children will die. It is destined, but should not be looked upon with despair; most choose to die, and are welcomed into the Temple of the Teacher Prophets.

Without the sacrifice of the willing, the Avatar will not be born into a land of peace. Perhaps the Avatar will not be born at all; it is unclear. That ten thousand is the number, it is certain. Ten thousand must die.

Kira read it again, then closed her eyes. There were over a thousand documented prophetic writings accepted by the Vedek Assembly and the Chamber of Ministers as having been influenced by the Prophets, easily several thousand more that had been rejected; Istani Reyla would surely have taken it before the Assembly, if she'd actually believed that it was real. Or to a vedek, at the very least. Ro could have read exaggerated importance into a few vague predictions . . . and even as complicated as a twenty-plus-millennia-old book would be to create, it surely wasn't impossible.

Kira felt new ache. The idea that the sweet and compassionate Reyla might have been murdered over some kind of a fraud scheme, something so useless, so trivial, was a dismal one. It made her wish that the clumsy killer were still alive, so that she could kill him herself.

If it *was* true . . . but no, with the seeds of doubt planted, she couldn't swallow it. Not without reading it herself, first.

I should *get back to bed.* The station repairs were unfinished, their defenses unreliable, and the Allied task force would be coming within the next twenty to thirty hours, give or take, planning to charge into the Gamma Quadrant to see what the Dominion was really up to. It was a decision that no one on the station agreed with, whether or not they could get DS9 operational in time to defend against the probable outcome; the task force was a bad idea.

The Allies feared that the isolated strike on the station was a Dominion ploy; Kitana'klan, their Jem'Hadar mystery guest, claimed that the Founders hadn't sanctioned the attack. She wanted to believe it . . . but Kitana'klan could be lying. It didn't help that the station's internal sensors were still uncertain, and the manual sweeps were inconclusive; for all they knew, there could be a dozen more of the damned soldiers lurking around, and one was already over Kira's limit.

Kira had more than enough insanity to deal with without crediting a probable forgery . . . but she couldn't dismiss it, not yet. If Ro was as right as *she* thought she was, they were headed for a very dark place.

Sighing, Kira touched the command that sent the translation back to its beginning and started to read.

Jake piloted the shuttle *Venture* back toward the station, carefully watching the radiation levels that hid his approach. He was probably being overly cautious; Nog had said that the destruction of the *Aldebaran* had irradiated the station's immediate vicinity, making it nearly impossible to detect a ship—certainly a personal shuttle the size of the *Venture*—but Jake wanted to be sure that he couldn't be tracked.

The departure log would show that he'd left DS9 headed for the most common route to Earth, assuming anyone wanted to look, and if what Nog had said was true, the sensors shouldn't be able to pick up his return.

Or me going into the wormhole, if I'm careful. And lucky. He'd been incredibly lucky already; the circumstances couldn't be better, with so much of the station still being repaired or upgraded, and the wormhole still being triggered by remnants of the *Aldebaran.* Once the Federation showed up, they'd start investigating the wreckage, then transporting the remains away. That would close his window of opportunity; once they arrived, there'd be no way for him to get into the wormhole undetected.

He was still out of sensor range, but could see the tiny dot of DS9 on the viewscreen, and even imagined that he could see the cloud of destruction that billowed near the station, an invisible aura of hazardous energy studded with great, ragged pieces of the *Aldebaran.*

Although there were at least seven ship remnants large enough for what he had planned, there were only two that seemed to be on a trajectory that would trigger the wormhole. Jake meant to ease in behind one of them, carefully keeping it between him and the station as he fired a couple of low-power thruster bursts to help it along, low enough that the radiation should cloak him completely. The Klingon patrol ship, the *Tcha'voth,* might spot some of the energy bleed, but they were guarding against attack *from* the Gamma Quadrant; they'd go with the station's assessment in the end, because the bleed would dissipate too fast to be coming from a cloaked ship. A frag trigger explained things nicely.

And then I'll find him. I'll find him and bring him home.

The thought gave him flutters of anxious hope. He knew the prophecy almost by heart, of course, but it was a comfort to see it, to hold it in his hands; keeping an eye on the *Venture*'s careful progress, Jake reached down into his bag and pulled out the small bundle that Istani Reyla had given to him. It seemed like a million years ago, but it had been less than a week—and the prylar had been killed only days after their meeting, a fact that Jake still hadn't fully digested. He focused instead on the ancient page of writing that he unwrapped, that told him what he had to do.

Jake traced the symbols of the dead language, the words of the translation clear in his mind, the parchment waxy and soft beneath his trembling fingers.

> *A Herald, unforgotten but lost to time and removed from sight, a Seer of Visions to whom the Teacher Prophets sing, will return from the Temple at the end of this time to attend the birth of New Hope, the Infant Avatar. The welcomed Herald shares a new understanding of the Temple with all the land's children. Conceived by lights of war, the alien Avatar opens its eyes upon a waxing tide of Awareness.*
>
> *The journey to the land hides, but is difficult; prophecies are revealed and hidden. The first child, a son, enters the Temple alone. With the Herald, he returns, and soon after, the*

Avatar is born. A new breath is drawn and the land rejoices in change and clarity.

Herald. Or Emissary. And who else could the first son be, if the Avatar was Kas and Dad's baby? Istani Reyla had given the prophecy to him because she knew that it was true, and he knew it, too. He could feel it, and that everything had gone so smoothly—buying the *Venture* from Quark, the readiness with which everyone had bought his story about going to Earth to visit his grandfather, even the fact that the *Aldebaran* had been destroyed and would effectively shield his movements—all of it had fit together in a way that was almost frightening, that suggested there were greater powers at work. Powers that wanted him to succeed.

Except for Istani Reyla, his mind whispered. *Where did she fit in?*

He didn't know, and didn't want to think about it. At the moment, there was nothing he could do about it anyway, not without abandoning his mission. When he got back, he'd tell Kira everything, he'd tell her about the prophecy and what he suspected—that somehow, Istani had been killed because of it.

Or I'll tell Dad. He'll know what to do.

It was hope talking, but that was okay; he thought he deserved a little hope. And if he was wrong about everything, no one would ever have to know what he had attempted. He could make up a story about the shuttle being faulty, that it had been nudged into the wormhole by some of the debris as he was returning to the station; he could make up anything he liked, if the prophecy turned out to be false.

It won't be.

On the screen, the space station slowly grew, its tiny lights glittering and bright against the fathomless dark. Jake tucked the aged paper back into its wrapping, excited and nervous. He was going to bring his father home.

2

Captain Picard found Elias Vaughn in cargo hold D, standing over the closed ark that held the Orb of Memory. It didn't surprise him, really; the commander had been quite taken with the Bajoran artifact. Understandably.

Vaughn glanced up as Picard approached, perhaps pulled from his reverie by the sound of another's footsteps. The cargo hold was still and peaceful, the low lights making it seem even quieter, a dark and silent place far from the bustle of a starship.

"Captain," Vaughn said lightly, tilting his head. "You're up early this morning."

"Commander," Picard returned, smiling. "Yes. I hope I haven't interrupted your—meditation, but I thought you might like to join Dr. Crusher and myself for breakfast. It may be our last chance." They were running a few hours late on original estimates, but if nothing else went wrong with their engines, they'd now reach DS9 in just over fourteen hours. Picard expected that the commander would take a shuttle to Starbase 375, to whatever new assignment awaited him, once they'd concluded their business at the station.

Vaughn smiled back at him, but seemed distracted. "Kind of you to ask, Jean-Luc, but I'm not actually hungry. It's a little too early for me . . . or late, rather."

Picard hesitated, not sure if Vaughn was asking him to leave or inviting further conversation. The man he'd known as Elias Vaughn had always kept his own counsel, not secretive so much as reserved, although he surely had his secrets—a Starfleet officer with an eighty-year career in strategic operations had probably forgotten more clandestine information than Picard would ever know.

But after his Orb experience, Elias had seemed renewed in spirit, an enthusiasm and openness to his manner that hadn't existed before. He'd described to Picard a sense of rediscovered purpose, and he had fairly glowed with it. Deanna had equated it to a spiritual awakening of sorts, a shift of his fundamental perceptions.

Vaughn was gazing down at the ark, the lines of his face now drawn into an unreadable mask. Picard continued to be intrigued by Vaughn's change in manner, but he wasn't one to pry; he had just decided to leave when the commander spoke, his strong voice soft in the still air.

"Strange things happen, Jean-Luc. Things that can't be explained away. That you know will probably never be explained."

Picard nodded. "I agree."

Vaughn grinned, and shook his head as he looked up from the ark. "It's nice to meet another realist. As long as we're agreeing on philosophical matters, I have a hypothetical question for you, a kind of moral dilemma."

Picard folded his arms. "How hypothetical?"

"Completely," Vaughn said. "Say that a high-ranking officer on your ship had received classified information about upcoming circumstances."

Picard nodded. Before they'd lost their subspace array, the commander had received several coded transmissions while on board.

"Say that the information regarded a space station, that your ship might now be headed for," Vaughn said, looking down at the ark again. "And say that this officer believes that if communications were working, you would have heard a declassified version by now. Unfortunately, you won't have the subspace relays operational before you get to the station. And the officer doesn't know what he *can* tell you, beyond the simplest of recommendations."

The charade of the hypothetical was obviously cursory on Vaughn's part, as if he'd only bothered with it at all to get their conversation started. Picard nodded again, stepping carefully. "Would this information be about anything that could jeopardize the safety of my crew, or this ship?"

"Chances are extremely low," Vaughn said. "You'd want to be on guard, that's all. You'll be able to talk to Starfleet about any possibly developing concerns once you reach the station."

Vaughn met his gaze, then, his own clear and perfectly reasonable, matter-of-fact . . . and it occurred to Picard that Vaughn was violating an entire career's worth of security status just to tell him that he should be wary. However else the Orb had affected him, he had clearly shifted his priorities regarding Starfleet.

"Dust is settling, Jean-Luc, that's all," Vaughn said.

Picard nodded, relaxing a bit even as he began reorganizing his own priorities. The kind of dust that settled after a war was fairly consistent, at least, everything that Vaughn said suggesting a minor skirmish, or perhaps another semi-organized protest by non-Federation activists. Almost inevitably from Alpha Quadrant worlds that hadn't been touched by the Dominion, their "passive" resistance had included some minor sabotage to a few Starfleet vessels, all performed on ships docked at non-Federation stations.

Supplement shield emitters, engineering and tactical to yellow, reinforce security procedures before docking . . . They would arrive at DS9 around 2100 hours ship time, but their plans for a midrange maintenance layover might be subject to change, depending on what had happened. Vaughn didn't seem to think it was too serious, but he wouldn't have warned him without cause, either.

"I think I will take you up on that breakfast," Vaughn said abruptly. "We have a busy day ahead, don't we?"

"That we do," Picard said, as they left the hold together, the captain noting that Vaughn's gaze lingered on the Orb for as long as it was still in sight.

". . . and Ezri *recommended* that he be moved to one of the cargo bays, so he wouldn't feel like a prisoner," Nog said. "And when I asked her about it last night, she started on about building *trust,* and getting him some privacy. There are only two guards posted outside, *two.* Like there's any chance that a Jem'Hadar soldier isn't planning to kill us all, like he could ever be trusted. Can you believe it?" Just saying it out loud filled him with a renewed sense of angry betrayal; no one was taking the threat seriously. Nog shook his head in disgust.

Vic Fontaine sighed, running a hand through his rumpled hair. They sat on the couch in the singer's hotel suite, the first glimmers of a holographic dawn forming outside the holographic balcony. It was early, but Nog had hardly been able to sleep, too angry, and his first shift started at 0630; he needed to talk about that—that *creature,* and with Jake having run off to Earth and Ezri siding with the enemy, waking up Vic had seemed like the best choice.

"That's rough, pallie," Vic said, yawning, pulling his robe tighter as he stood up. "Listen, I'm going to order up coffee, maybe an omelet, side of home fries—you want anything?"

He wasn't positive about "home fries," but Nog remembered what an Earth-style omelet was made from, from his time at Starfleet Academy—bird eggs and flavored mold. In a word, revolting. How his father had ever developed a taste for the stuff was beyond him. He shook his head as Vic stepped to the phone, a little hurt that Vic hadn't reacted much to the news.

He knows *what they did to me,* he thought . . . but also remembered that Vic had never dealt with Jem'Hadar; he didn't understand what they were like.

Vic returned to the couch and flopped down. "Sorry, kid, I don't mean to be a drag. You know how I am mornings . . . and we did two encores last night," he said, shaking his head with a little smile. "My axeman—you know Dickie—he was trying to impress this skirt, a real looker, so we ran through the whole shebang. They were making eyes like you wouldn't believe. He made some points, though, got her number and a date for next week. Got to keep the boys happy, right?"

Nog nodded, deciphering the slang easily as Vic talked. It took some getting used to, but he thought he was probably better at it than anyone else on the station. When he had stayed with Vic for a few weeks, he used to love watching people tap anxiously at their translators when they entered the program. The universals didn't have much memory for period slang.

"So this Kitana'klan," Vic said casually. "Have you actually talked to him?"

"No! Are you kidding?" Even thinking about it terrified Nog, his palms suddenly spiked with sweat, although he did his best to bluster his way through. "I don't have anything to say to a Jem'Hadar. They're bred to kill, it's all they know how to do. And it seems like everyone suddenly forgot that, like they forgot how many people died because of them."

Vic nodded, but didn't look convinced. "Way I heard it, he had a chance to hurt a lot of people when he was hiding out," the singer said lightly. "And that he didn't put up a racket when you and Shar and the doc found him . . . maybe everyone thinks this one's different because—"

"He's not," Nog interrupted, hardly able to credit

what he was hearing, feeling his ears flush with hurt and disbelief. "He was on one of those attack ships, Vic! I can't prove it, but he can't prove that he wasn't, either! Why is everyone so ready to believe him?"

"Easy, kid, easy," Vic said soothingly, raising his hands in conciliatory surrender. "You gotta remember that most folks are ready to put the war behind them. And this guy turns up saying that Odo sent him, and that the attack on the station was a fluke, and that the Dominion has hung up its gloves and wants to make nice. I'm sure a lot of people feel like you do about it, it's just—they're tired, that's all."

Nog nodded slowly, frustrated but thinking he could understand being tired. When the Jem'Hadar on AR-558 had blown off his leg, when he'd run from the reality of the war into Vic Fontaine's innocuous and engrossing world, there had been times he'd woken up in the small hours and lain there, remembering, over and over, staring at the ceiling that wasn't really there, his new leg aching. Struggling with his first real understanding of his own mortality, a terrible gift given to him by the Jem'Hadar. The faces of dead Federation soldiers fresh in his mind, in the dark . . .

I was so tired then that I couldn't leave the holosuite. The same kind of deliberate ignorance to reality as the people he'd talked to last night at Uncle's; it made sense when he thought about it. They *wanted* to believe Kitana'klan's story, because the alternative was to consider new deception by the Dominion. And no one wanted to think about the Dominion at all.

"So what do I do?" Nog asked, his anger subsiding to a grudging understanding of what he was up against.

"If you think he's bad news, kid, you stick to your guns," Vic said firmly. "Talk to some more people, find out how the scene is sitting with them. Stay cool, though, try to keep in mind that everyone has a right to an opinion . . . and keep your eyes open."

There was a knock at the door, presumably Vic's breakfast. Nog and Vic both stood up, Nog finding a smile for his friend.

"I have to get to work," Nog said. "But—thanks, Vic. I feel better. Sorry about waking you up."

Vic smiled back. "Anytime, kid. I mean that; I still owe you for rent."

Nog held his breath as he brushed past room service, a young simulated hew-mon holding a steaming plate of noxious food, and headed for the exit, feeling stronger about his position. It was a relief to know that at least one other person on the station hadn't lost his reason. Nog wasn't overreacting; everyone else was *underreacting.*

Kitana'klan was bad news, no doubt about it, and Nog also had no doubt that behind that scaly, spiky face was a mind calculating how to destroy them all.

Ezri nodded at the guards outside the cargo bay, shifting the two staffs she carried as she approached the door, praying that she wasn't making a huge mistake.

No. Trust has to start somewhere, and this is as good a beginning as any. She hoped.

Yesterday's initial interview with Kitana'klan had given her very little to work with; he had only repeated the story he gave Kira, that he had been sent by Odo to act as a kind of cultural observer on behalf of the Jem'Hadar. Of the four strike ships that had come through the wormhole, he claimed to be the pilot of the one ship that had tried to protect DS9 from the other three, all supposedly rogue Jem'Hadar fighters. He said he'd transported to the station even as his ship was destroyed, and remained shrouded for fear that his motives would be suspect following the attack.

It was a good story, and it certainly explained a lot. If it was true, if the Dominion wasn't behind the attack, then there was no need for the Allies to send a battle-ready fleet into the Gamma Quadrant. If he was lying, he was an enemy.

Which means it all comes down to whether or not I *can figure out if he's telling the truth. No pressure, Ezri.* Her inner voice sounded a bit amused; she was actually eager to see how her rapidly evolving self-image would affect her insight.

A few deep breaths and she nodded at one of the two security guards, who tapped at a control panel, unlocking the bay. The door slid open and a second guard, Corporal Devro, preceded her inside, phaser drawn.

Ezri had to admit to herself that she was relieved to have an escort. Fear wasn't the issue; the extra set of eyes meant she could relax more, to start seeing how he said the things he said, to try and get a better understanding of his capabilities. There wasn't enough known about Jem'Hadar behavioral psychology for her to assume much of anything.

And Julian will certainly be glad to know I didn't

do this alone. He had expressed some concern with her new assignment, although he hadn't pushed, not with the current tension between them. They weren't fighting, but they weren't talking enough, either . . .

. . . *and now is* definitely *not the time.* Ezri cleared her mind, feeling the whole of her come into balance.

The Jem'Hadar soldier stood in the middle of the cavernous bay, empty except for a few stacks of broken-down storage containers and some shelving. As instructed, Devro remained near the door as Ezri approached the Jem'Hadar, still holding the two staffs. Each was about two meters long, made from a light but dense alloy—a sparring weapon with a decent heft, common to many martial and physical arts. Jem'Hadar fought, it was what they did, and although she wasn't as physically capable as some of her predecessors, she thought she could hold her own with Kitana'klan in an exercise. Long enough to earn his respect, anyway.

The staffs were safer than *bat'leths,* or the Jem'Hadar's usual blade weapon of choice, the *kar'takin* . . . but she wasn't going to kid herself; a Jem'Hadar could kill with whatever was at hand. She was counting on the fact that, whether he was telling the truth or not, it would be against his purpose to kill her here and now.

She stopped in front of Kitana'klan, who looked down at her with an absolutely unreadable expression. As usual. He hadn't expressed any emotion that she had understood, although Kira said he'd been quite adamant about swearing his loyalty to her, even offering the colonel his ketracel-white cartridge. As long as they had white, Jem'Hadar didn't need food or sleep to survive, but they died horribly if their supply of the enzyme ran out. Most of the time, at least; she knew that Julian had once met a soldier who could survive without white, but he had been a genetic anomaly.

"I thought you might be restless," she said, carefully keeping her expression neutral. "My last host once trained with some Jem'Hadar for a joint mission, before the war. So I'm familiar with a few of your hand-to-hand combat drills." She tossed him a staff, and he scarcely moved as he picked it out of the air with one hand. "Let's dance."

He hefted the staff with one hand, not taking his dark, ambiguous gaze from hers. From what she knew about them, Jem'Hadar were both intelligent and inquisitive. They also responded to directness, and Ezri hoped that by challenging him to a physical contest, she would finally make meaningful contact.

"Agreed," Kitana'klan said, and backed up a step, crouching slightly.

Ezri held her staff loosely in both hands, one hand facing up, watching as he took a few sliding steps to his right. He held his staff the same way, suggesting that he was familiar with the weapon . . . or maybe for a Jem'Hadar it was instinctive, coded into their genetic sequencing. Neither would surprise her.

Ezri summoned up all of her Starfleet combat training. Then she reached within herself, first to Jadzia's experience battling Jem'Hadar on Vandros IV, then to her sparring sessions with Worf. She tapped into Curzon's lifelong study of the *mok'bara,* and further back still to Emony's athletic prowess. She then extended her awareness outward, reaching with her senses to take in all of her opponent; his face and body, stance, which muscles were flexed. The chest and the waist were crucial; staff action would begin in one of those two areas. Looking into your opponent's eyes was a mistake, a look could be faked, and Kitana'klan certainly knew—

—*slap,* a blur of motion, and the back of her right hand was stinging, the move so fast that he was already back and away as she registered the pain.

Uh-oh.

She nodded in acknowledgment, startled and not a little impressed; he could have broken her fingers just as easily.

They circled, Ezri turning off her consciousness as much as she could, letting her observations take its place. What she thought wasn't important, because it didn't matter; the first rule of Galeo-Manada was not to worry about what your opponent might do, but to flow with what he or she *did* do.

Except Jadzia was the wrestler, not me—

—relax, dammit!

She was Ezri, and their memories were hers. She held the staff at a slight angle in front of her body, watching and waiting, circling as he did. She had no plans to attack, for physical as well as psychological considerations; he was better than her, obviously, but she also thought an attack by her might reinforce his negative beliefs about—

—a thrust, aimed at her gut. Ezri parried, knocking the staff down and away, but it was an effort. He was strong. It was all she could do to avoid his follow-through—

—and as he leaned into his thrust, Ezri spun into

her dodge, wheeling around and raising her staff for a blow to his shoulder, but he was already gone. He'd stepped away, moving faster than any being she'd ever fought, only a breeze across her face.

She continued the turn, putting a leap into her spin as he stepped back into her range, crouching even lower, *feint for his head and come in low—*

—and in a single, brutal movement, Kitana'klan raised his staff with incredible force, knocking her own out of one hand. She lost her balance for a split second, but it was all he needed—if he even needed that to beat her. He brought the staff around, low, sweeping her feet out from under her, the weighted stick cracking painfully against the side of her left ankle.

She went down, slapping the ground with her free hand, vaguely aware that the security officer was shouting something. The light was blocked, Kitana'klan towering over her, staff aimed for her throat—

—his eyes, look at them—

—and she felt the cold metal tap at her windpipe, so slightly that it was almost a tickle. The Jem'Hadar stepped back, lowering his staff.

"It's okay!" Ezri called, breathing deeply as she sat up, afraid that young Corporal Devro might open fire. Kitana'klan looked down at her, his face as blank as ever as he reached out to help her up.

"You fight well," he said, his voice without inflection.

"You lie poorly," she said. "I respect your greater skill, and appreciate your mercy. Perhaps we can talk, once I put away these weapons."

Kitana'klan nodded dismissively. Ezri collected

both staffs, thinking of how he'd looked at her, thinking of the killing rage she'd seen in his eyes at her moment of complete vulnerability. He hadn't just wanted to kill her; he'd *craved* it.

He's Jem'Hadar, he can't help what he is. And he could have easily done it, if he wanted to. He restrained himself, that's what matters.

Another mental voice, just as loud. *Of course he restrained himself, killing me would only hurt his situation. He didn't strike because he has other plans.*

She didn't know what to think. All she knew was that she wasn't going to plan any more therapeutic sparring sessions, certainly not any in which she was an active participant. However positive she was feeling about her other skills, Kitana'klan was clearly superior in a fight . . . and that look in his eyes . . .

She had her opening to ask questions, it was what she'd wanted. Aware that he was watching her, she did her best not to limp as she walked to the door, Devro covering her. Kitana'klan simply stood there, needing nothing from any of them.

3

It was time to enter the wormhole.

The *Venture* had been floating in the shadow of a massive section of hull from the lost *Aldebaran,* on the off chance that the wormhole was being visually monitored . . . and according to his shuttle's course reads, it was very close. Close enough that he shouldn't have to do any more than tap the piece with his shields.

This is crazy, Jake thought, manually setting the controls to ease the shuttle forward, wondering what his friends would think of what he was doing, knowing that his father would understand. It was a charge from a prophecy that Jake wholly believed, because his heart told him it was true; how could he possibly do anything but try to fulfill it?

You could have stayed on the station, he told himself. *You could have talked it over with someone a little more objective. You could have helped your friends deal with their losses, helped with the inves-*

tigation into Istani Reyla's murder, helped Nog deal with having a Jem'Hadar on board—

"It's a little late for that now," he murmured, unblinking, his gaze glued to the navigation screen—

—and a funnel of swirling energy blossomed around the tiny shuttle. He felt a trickle of sweat run down his back, hands on manual, hoping that his good luck would hold, that he could have just another few seconds as the *Venture* edged incrementally through the wormhole's brilliant entrance. Hoping that he wasn't about to totally humiliate himself in the process of botching his mission.

Help me, Dad, help this to happen.

And then he had crossed the threshold.

Nog was watching his boards in ops with only half an eye, working up another repair-time estimate on the *Defiant,* when the sensor alerts flashed. Tactical and science jumped to attention.

Nog put the wormhole on the main screen before Lieutenant Bowers could ask for it. A frozen field of debris was illuminated across the screen, standing in harsh silhouette contrast to the blinding beauty of the lights.

"No trails, no increase in energized particle count . . . and I'm not reading any displacement in the field," Shar said, and Nog realized he'd been holding his breath when he blew it out in a rush. Another fragment.

"It *is* one we were tracking . . ." Shar continued, his long fingers running across science's control board. "But it shouldn't have tripped the entrance yet, not for another three hours, twenty minutes. It wasn't moving fast enough."

"Is the disparity within a reasonable range, counting for probable collision factors?" Bowers asked.

"Affirmative."

Bowers nodded, looking relieved. Nog didn't blame him; Colonel Kira had called in to say she had some other business to see to before coming up, which meant the lieutenant would have had to make any necessary split-second decisions. It wasn't a responsibility that any of them wanted, not with how things currently stood.

"Communications, contact the *Tcha'voth* and see if our readings match up," Bowers said.

Looks like we're not being invaded quite yet, Nog thought, smiling uneasily at Shar and shrugging. Shar nodded, composed as always. Nog had always heard that Andorians didn't succumb to pressure as easily as others, that they actually got even calmer in crisis situations—until they got violent, anyway. As if he needed any more proof, after the way Shar had handled the Jem'Hadar at Quark's. . . .

"Ah, they say they might have a signature reading—" Shoka Pian, at communications, her terse voice snapping Nog back to attention.

Shoka placed one hand to her earpiece, listening, everyone in ops watching her. She was a volunteer from Bajor, a Militia communications consultant who had shuttled in with some of the engineers to help fill in shifts. Nog strained to hear what was being said, but could only hear a tinny crackling sound.

"—wait, they've lost it," she said, her tone relaxing. "If it was there, it's gone now."

Bowers smiled. "Because they were picking up residuals off the fragment. Again. Please ask them to continue monitoring, unless they wish to pursue the possible reading."

They wouldn't. Nog swallowed heavily, wondering how many more of these they had to look forward to before the Federation showed up. Sciences said only two more ship fragments would trigger the wormhole, but they obviously weren't perfect. He felt bad, thinking of the *Aldebaran* as some kind of nuisance, but the station's tension level was high enough without surprise wormhole openings.

Nog picked up his *Defiant* report again, his stomach a little fluttery, thinking of how much he despised the Dominion and their damned soldiers for teaching him to be so afraid.

Ro had slept poorly, half listening for the computer's voice to tell her that the colonel was calling. Kira finally contacted her just as Ro was getting dressed for her morning shift, asking her to come to the security office.

Ro hurried to get ready, wondering if Kira had already contacted Bajor's provisional government, wondering who else might be waiting in her office. A vedek or two, maybe someone from the First Chamber. She ran her fingers through her hair as she left her quarters, not really caring how she looked but wanting to appear sane, at least.

Ro had no idea what anyone could possibly do to prevent a prophecy from happening, but imagined that it would be handled like a natural disaster of some kind. She had given it a lot of thought while not sleeping. As far as she was concerned, the wormhole aliens weren't gods—but no one could deny that they possessed godlike powers. And there were too many actualized prophecies in Bajoran history to ignore one this specific, not with the entire book to back it up.

She was a little surprised to see only Kira waiting for her at the door, holding the cloth-wrapped book and its translation in one arm. Her expression was impassive, and she looked tired. They stepped into the office together, Ro thinking that she might learn to get along with Kira, after all. She took her job seriously, which Ro could respect.

The thought was wiped away with Kira's first words.

"It's not valid," she said, holding the items out to Ro, actually smiling a little. "I'll admit, I was a little scared reading this, at first; there are several writings in here that are incredibly close to actual historical events. But the Prophets didn't have anything to do with this."

Ro took the book and the padd, frowning. "How do you know? What did the lab find out about its age?"

Kira's smile faded. "I didn't take it to the lab. I know because of the content."

Ro stared at her, not sure what she was hearing. "In what way?"

"In that the Prophets never Touched the person or persons who wrote this book," Kira said, as though she were stating some kind of fact. "Who was obviously insane. And it's too obvious, with just enough metaphorical twisting to make it seem halfway credible. It's fallacious and heretical."

Ro had known that the devout Kira wasn't going to like the book's secular theme, but had convinced herself that when it got down to it, the colonel would do the right thing—that she would know the truth when she saw it, and act accordingly. Ro had also considered the possibility that the book was an elaborate fake, written for some unknown purpose, but she seriously doubted it—although until they had it looked over by an expert, there was no way to be sure.

Now she opened her mouth to tell Kira who the insane one obviously was, but realized that what she was going to blurt out would shut the conversation down before it even got started. She snapped her mouth shut, counted three, and tried not to seem furious. She was a thread from losing her patience.

"Did you read all of the translation?" Ro asked. "Because there were some very unclear parts, but—"

"I read all of it," Kira interrupted. "I know you're not . . . one of the faithful, Ro, but I've read every accepted prophecy, some from the same era as this book—and there's no mention of anything like this, or any acknowledgment of this prophecy being made. The Prophets would never ask for anyone to die, or condone it as destiny. They convey messages of life, not visions of death."

It was Kira's tone that did it, the faintest hint of gentle sympathy for poor, faithless Ro. The thread snapped.

"Are you being deliberately ignorant?" Ro asked, words spilling out sharp and fast, angry disbelief lending heat to her voice. "Everything in that book has happened, and you don't think it's a fake any more than I do. Just because it hasn't been verified by some religious *authority* doesn't make it any less true, it doesn't change what's in the book, and excuse me, but don't you think it's a little presumptuous for you to decide what the Prophets would or would not condone?"

She had stepped over the line, but barely cared. Kira had too much responsibility to indulge her religious biases; it wasn't appropriate and it was maddening, besides.

High color flooded Kira's cheeks. In contrast to the fire in Ro that had made her snap, that bloomed even now in the colonel's face, Kira's manner was deep-space cold.

"Give it to me," she said, thrusting one hand out. "I'm turning it over to Vedek Yevir, to take to the Assembly. If they say it's authentic, we'll move from there. And if not, they have enough experience with false prophecies to take suitable action."

Denounce it loudly, of course. And then maybe set it on fire.

Ro turned and placed the book and translation on her desk before answering, aware that she was probably about to be dismissed from duty as she faced Kira again.

"This book is a key piece of evidence in an ongoing murder investigation," Ro said, keeping her tone as even as she could. "Once the investigation is over, you can lay a claim to it; until then, it stays here."

She hurried on before Kira could respond, just trying to get some kind of point across, something that would make the colonel reconsider her position. "If the artifact *is* genuine, do you think the Vedek

Assembly is the only Bajoran group who should have access? You know it's from B'hala, it has to be, which means it belongs to everyone. Do you honestly believe that the Assembly will even consider keeping it as a historical document, let alone opening any part of it to debate?"

Kira didn't seem to be listening. She looked at Ro with something like pity, but her voice carried that no-nonsense tone of absolute belief that to Ro, at least, represented the dogma of the pietistic.

"I don't expect you to understand."

Never underestimate the power of faith. Ro hated that one. It was a tenet of the shrine, as if faith were *always* a good thing.

"But I *do* expect a bare minimum of respect, as the commanding officer of this station," Kira said, meeting Ro's gaze squarely. "Think of it as a courtesy, if you'd rather, but don't forget it if you want to continue working here."

Ro looked away. She was still angry, but Kira was right about that much. She was too old to be indulging her temper, having long seen it as one of her shortcomings.

"Yes, Colonel."

Kira nodded briskly. "Fine. I'll expect a progress report on your pending research results this afternoon, in person. We can talk about a few other matters then, too."

"Are you going to show it to Captain Yates?" Ro asked, her voice flat with resignation. Without the colonel's support, there would be no independent investigation into the book, except for how it related to Istani's murder. Whatever happened, Yates should know that she was an indirect part of the investigation before anyone else did.

Kira seemed startled by the question. "I suppose I should," she said, after a brief hesitation. She reached past Ro and picked up the translation padd. "Is there anything else, Lieutenant?"

Ro shook her head, and Kira turned and walked out without another word. Ro stared after her for a moment, then sat down at her desk, crossing her arms and leaning back in her chair. She gazed absently at the book, thinking, frustrated and alarmed by the situation, surprised at how leniently Kira had responded to her outburst; if their positions had been reversed, Ro would certainly have dismissed her.

Mostly she thought of how comforting it must be, to really believe that the Prophets held every Bajoran in their all-encompassing hands, that they saw every Bajoran as a child to be loved and guided. It had its advantages . . . not the least of which being that if she really did believe, she'd be able to dismiss the book as easily as Kira had.

Ro sighed and turned to the morning security reports, still not sure if she truly belonged on DS9.

4

Kasidy was sitting at the small desk in her quarters' living room, revising a list of things to do for her stay at the house. She wasn't leaving for another two days, and would only be staying on Bajor for three, but she loved making lists. Having moved to part-time with the Commerce Ministry, she had a lot of free time to "putter," as her grandmother had liked to say—make lists, catch up on correspondence, take naps.

And eat, she thought sheepishly, glancing over at the small stack of empty plates on the table. Boy or girl, it was going to come out the size of a four-year-old if it didn't slow down.

. . . see about hiring field equipment for spring, check vineyard possibilities(?), check new channel reception . . . This would probably be her last short trip before the move, and she wanted to be organized, to make sure that she took care of as many house details as possible. Jake would probably be

back in time to help her unpack, but she'd like to keep the move as stress-free as possible for both of them. He missed his father a lot, she could see it in him every time they talked about the house or the baby, and she wanted to spend a few days with him just being friends. Puttering.

She was seriously debating whether or not to order up another plate of gingerbread when her door signaled. It was Nerys, just in time to save her.

"Come in," Kas called, standing. "Good morning! Did you get enough sleep? You were still at Quark's when I left, and that had to be after 2400 sometime."

"Did Jake really leave?" Kira asked. "Nog told me he did, but I haven't actually looked at the departure list since last night."

Kas smiled, shaking her head. "Well, you know Jake and the limelight. That, and I got the feeling he was in a big hurry to get to Earth."

Kira nodded, but didn't seem to be listening. Kas noticed she was holding a padd at her side, and seemed a little edgy.

She doesn't want to tell me something.

"So what brings you by this morning?" Kas asked, dropping one hand to her lower belly without even thinking about it.

Her nervousness must have showed. "Kas, it's probably nothing at all, really," Kira said, and Kasidy tensed even further. "Let's sit down, all right? There's a story."

Kas sat, and Kira explained. Kira's lost friend, the monk, had been carrying a book with her when she came to the station, and had hidden it soon after arriving. Ro Laren had found the hiding place—coincidentally, less than ten meters from Kas's door—and believed that there was a chance the book had something to do with the murderer's motive for killing Istani Reyla.

Kas's initial unease slowly deepened—it was as though a part of her had expected this, had been waiting for it. As soon as the word "prophecy" cropped up, she had to interrupt, ready to get it over with.

"Is it a prophecy about Ben?" Kas asked, afraid that it was . . . but even more afraid that it wasn't. *Not the baby, please, not the baby—*

"Kasidy, listen to me—I don't believe that anything in the book can be verified as coming from a credible—"

"Nerys, *tell me,*" Kas interrupted, really starting to worry.

"One of these alleged prophecies says that your baby will be an important figure in the lives of the Bajoran faithful," Kira said, quietly and directly. "And although I absolutely believe the entire book is a fake, I thought you should know."

Kas was nodding, trying to accept what she was saying, her heart pounding. Her baby, the little somebody who liked ginger and made it hard to sleep comfortably, whom she already loved and was committed to, a religious figure for the Bajorans.

You knew this was a possibility when you got married, take a breath. She'd had the wonderful but rotten luck to fall in love with the Emissary, after all, and had come to a slow, careful acceptance of what that entailed . . . for herself. She'd avoided thinking about what would happen to the child of the Emissary, hoping the baby would take toward her side of the family. Her distinctly normal, pleasantly non-mystical family.

She thought she could deal with it. It wasn't what she wanted, but she understood that everything wasn't up to her. And she'd come to some very positive realizations about herself, about her feelings for the little somebody; she would protect her, or him. Kas had never been a violent person in any way, but in just a few weeks, she'd come to understand the capacity for it in her life—no one would hurt the baby, or they wouldn't be around long enough to regret being born.

"Okay," Kas said, still nodding, taking another deep breath. "Okay, it could be worse. What does it say, exactly?"

Kira held out the padd, presumably the translation to the book. "Kas, I think you should read it. I'm sure this is going to turn out to be some kind of elaborate hoax, to deceive an artifact collector, or extort gain somehow . . . but it may mean that you'll be in the public view again, until the official denunciation is made."

Kasidy took it from her, suddenly realizing that some of the tension in Kira's stance was from fear, whether she admitted it or not.

She's trying to convince me that it's not real, because she doesn't want to believe it, either.

"I've never known you to shy away from the truth, Nerys," Kas said softly. "What does it say?"

Kira hesitated, but must have realized that she wasn't making things any easier. "The book says there will be a sacrifice made before the birth, to ensure that everything will be ready when the baby comes," Kira replied, searching Kas's face for a response. "A Bajoran sacrifice."

Kasidy was starting to feel sick. "What? A person?"

"Ten thousand people."

Kas's fingers were numb, holding the padd. "Ten thousand Bajorans are supposed to die before the big miracle, is that right? Is that what you're telling me?"

"I'm telling you that either some unknown lunatic nonbeliever wrote that down a long time ago, or someone made it up entirely, Kas," Kira said firmly. "And now it's a piece of evidence in a criminal investigation, and that's the only context it belongs in."

Get away, protect the baby.

Kasidy made the decision as the words were leaving her mouth, giving over to a sudden surge of protective instinct. "I'm going to be moving sooner than I expected," she said. "I was planning on going to the property, anyway. To finish up, I mean."

To visit my new home, to finalize a few last details. On a planet that worships the beings who keep taking things from me, and the more I give, the more they demand. My husband, my peace of mind, a normal childhood for our baby.

Maybe she shouldn't be moving to Bajor at all.

"Kas, I'm going to resolve this as soon as I can," Kira said. "The investigation won't take more than another day, I'm sure. Ro is expecting some test results on Reyla's killer, to make an identification, and then it should be over. Please stay."

Kas was unhappy with all her choices, but it wasn't Kira's fault. And Kira had been a good friend to her, asking nothing in return for helping her make Ben's house a reality.

"I'll stay, but I want to read this," Kas said, looking down at the padd and then back at Kira again. "All of it. I need to know what else it says."

Kira nodded reluctantly, and stood up. "Of course. I should be in my office most of the day, if you want to talk."

After she'd gone, Kas stared at the padd for a long time, wishing there were someone to blame for such craziness, someone to hold responsible for the things that had happened in her life since she met Ben Sisko. He was worth it, she believed, most of the time; other times, she had to wonder.

After breakfast, Vaughn decided to see if there was a holodeck available. Picard had called for a senior staff meeting, probably to suggest a few defense adjustments, and Vaughn was feeling restless.

He was in luck, two rooms open. It was a luxury he rarely indulged in, holodeck time, generally preferring to read—but he'd decided over breakfast that he'd like to relax with his thoughts for a while. He felt a need to analyze some of what he'd been going through.

"Computer, do you have 'Life Cycle Meditation/Old Growth Forest'? Program number 06010, I think." Vaughn doubted the *Enterprise*-E would carry it; it was one of the earliest holoprograms.

"Affirmative."

"Run it," Vaughn said, smiling as he punched in his visitor code and a time call. It had been at least ten years since he'd used the program, but he'd thought about it several times since his experience with the Orb, remembering it wistfully.

He stepped onto the holodeck just as spring was

taking hold and started walking, wanting to get to the clearing before summer.

All around the trail that led into the thickly shaded woods, buds were forming on branches, flowers were springing up, saplings were becoming young trees. He saw a trio of baby rabbits, and heard fledgling birds crying. The sound and imagery were perfect.

By the time he reached the fully enclosed clearing he remembered, fresh young life was maturing. Plants were reaching their life peak, fuller and darker, their blossoms most brilliant, insects lazily buzzing past; half-grown animals darted through the trees, killing, mating, rolling on the ground in the sun. There was a sloping, grassy rise in the middle of the open space, a perfect place to sit; Vaughn flopped down comfortably, crossing his legs, watching as the forest evolved.

Summer, then fall, things dying, changing color, holing up for winter in small spaces. In the winters, it usually snowed. Vaughn didn't feel the cold air or the gentle sting of the snow, for the same reason it never got too dark to see, or some things grew disproportionately fast or moved disproportionately slow. The point of the program wasn't to simulate reality, or to simply show a speeded-up loop. It was a backdrop for meditation, the soft sounds becoming a drone of occurrences, nothing so jerky or loud as to distract attention from anything else.

He saw a white rabbit slaughtered by a white fox, then a thin deer, nosing for something to eat. He heard tree branches snapping, and thunder. And a moment later, the trickle of thaw, and a smattering of pale green crept up across the clearing. The forest evolved for about twenty years, the full program running over two hours.

Vaughn watched, letting his mind wander. Thinking that he was starting to settle into his new mindset, feeling less exuberant and more thoughtful about his future. Interesting, that he was enjoying his introspection as much as he'd enjoyed his initial flush of vitality. It seemed that being born-again young made everything interesting, the heaviness of his past dropping away like cut ballast; he felt like he was looking up and out after years of staring straight ahead.

Midsummer, the grasses weaving in a simulated wind. Vaughn was glad he'd decided to tell Picard that the environment at and around DS9 might be unstable. Jean-Luc was more of a straight arrow than Vaughn had ever been, but he was also the kind of captain who lived and died for his crew and ship, a mentality Vaughn respected. Picard had appreciated the warning, and it had cost him nothing.

And admit it—you enjoyed telling him because you weren't supposed to. Although he had more discretion in clearance matters than most admirals, the Vaughn of a week ago probably wouldn't have done it. Because Starfleet officers didn't do things like that, the chain of command broke down when people didn't do their jobs; it wasn't the *code.*

Vaughn got to smiling as the autumn rains started to fall once more. At the age of 101, he had decided to stray off the path of absolute righteousness and military ideology because . . . because he wanted to, and it turned out that wanting to was enough. The cycle playing out all around him reaffirmed his confidence, the feelings of clarity and contemplative objectivity. Life went on, whether he was fulfilled or not; why not do as he wished?

He thought about what had happened on the freighter just before he'd closed the ark, wondered how it was meaningful. Assuming that approaching the Orb hadn't caused hallucinations, why had Benjamin Sisko been there? Vaughn couldn't remember having ever seeing an image of him before, and there had been nothing familiar about him at the time. Was it coincidence, that he'd seen the missing captain standing beside the Orb, and that the *Enterprise* was now on her way to DS9, the station he'd commanded? Of course not. The files Vaughn had been able to access on Sisko had an extremely detailed report about the captain's disappearance, and where he was presumed to have gone; friends in high places, so to speak. Vaughn was very much looking forward to exploring the noncoincidence a little further, and to meeting some of the people who'd worked with Sisko.

And with what will be happening at the wormhole entrance in a day or so, unless things have changed. . . .

The tragedy behind it was too vast to contemplate for long, and he'd known a lifetime of such tragedies—misunderstandings, acts of revenge or simple malice that created more tragedy, by encouraging mistrust, by encouraging hate, always in the name of necessity. Vaughn didn't think it would come to that; he expected there to be a lot of chest-thumping for a few days among the Allied forces, but saner heads would certainly prevail in the end, no matter what the political climate. They simply didn't have the energy or the resources to consider anything else.

The seasons changed, and Vaughn stopped thinking after a while, the low, persistent hum of life lulling and sweet to his ears. Rot and rebirth and rot, hope springing eternal, the end always near. He'd never been much of a philosopher, but some things seemed pretty obvious.

They had decided to have lunch together in his quarters, Julian knowing the second she walked in that she was ready to talk. Her posture and a micro-expression of anxiety beneath her smile gave her away.

Don't push, let her get to it on her own.

Ezri picked up the plate of salad he'd already replicated for her and sat down on the couch across from him, her shoulders tight. He wished that he understood his own feelings better. He thought about what Vic had said about giving her space, and then about his own frustrations with Ezri's distancing tactics; she was going through some kind of an emotional change, and he wanted to be supportive, but she'd consistently avoided talking about it—and hadn't taken any great pains to consider his feelings in the matter, either. Which hurt.

Julian set his own untouched plate on the low table that separated them. "You okay?" he asked.

She nodded. "Still sorry about the other day, though," she said, and Julian relaxed a little.

"I am, too," he said.

"It must been so strange for you—"

"It really was," he said, relaxing a little more.

Ezri smiled. "I guess you've noticed that I've been

thinking about some things since the attack on the station."

"Since you saved the station," Julian said, smiling back at her.

Ezri nodded vigorously, grinning. "Exactly, that's exactly right," she said. "Since I took command of the *Defiant*. Julian, it was such an amazing feeling, tapping my memories for leadership qualities and finding them. It wasn't a decision, to take command; it was more like a . . . a reflex."

"My" memories. Not Jadzia's, or one of the other hosts.

"And as soon as the immediate danger was past, it really hit me," she continued. "I knew it before, logically, but I'd never really experienced the power of who I am now. Even when I drew from Joran's personality to help me in that murder investigation last year, I treated him as something separate and apart from me. Now, though . . ."

Julian nodded, happy for her excitement. "That's wonderful. So you're feeling . . . more *integrated,* if that's the right term."

"More integrated, more confident," she said. "In the last couple of days, I've started to get used to the idea, that I'm not limited to the life goals Ezri Tigan set for herself. Not that those were bad things—a nice home, a family, my own counseling center someday. It's just that I can be so much *more.*"

Julian felt his friendly objectivity slipping just a bit. "So, you don't want those things?"

Ezri shook her head. "It's not that, I *do* want those things, but I have so much to figure out first."

Still smiling, she reached over and took his hand,

squeezing it tightly. "You know I never prepared for this life, Julian. Ever since I was joined, I've been struggling to figure out who *I* am, trying to understand where Ezri fit in the totality of Dax. That first year, I honestly didn't know if I could survive as Ezri Dax, I felt like I was being crowded out by eight strangers whom I somehow knew as intimately as I knew Ezri Tigan. I didn't know what to do with them. And worse, I was in constant fear of what they'd do to me.

"But when I took command on the *Defiant,* I had this kind of emotional realization—that 'I' means so much more for a joined Trill. But I wasn't just thinking it, for the first time I really *felt* it—Ezri is all of them, and Dax, *and* who I was before I was joined."

She shook her head again, releasing has hand. "I've just come to realize that I've been given this incredible chance, to see beyond the reality I grew up believing—that fulfillment comes only through our relationships to others. I never realized how alone I was then, not even *considering* the internal relationships that being joined could create."

Julian felt himself tensing. He didn't want to drag her away from enjoying her new insights, but it was as though she'd forgotten the nature of their relationship . . . and was continuing to overlook his feelings, about what had happened during their lovemaking, in what she was saying now. Being in bed with her, looking down to see Ezri open her eyes, to see Jadzia looking back up at him . . . he couldn't think of a word to describe how it had been, to feel that she had gone away and left him so vulnerable. That she had frightened him.

He kept his tone light, but couldn't entirely erase an edge from his words. "No more internal relationships sneaking up on me, I hope."

Ezri frowned, a half-smile still on her face. "What do you mean?"

"Nothing. It's just . . . the other night, I was caught off guard, and honestly, I'm not getting the feeling that you understand why that bothered me."

She wasn't smiling at all now. "I understand perfectly. And I said I was sorry, Julian. It wasn't like I planned it."

He could see the fight coming and he made a last effort to stop it. "I don't want to fight with you, Ezri. I love you. I just want you to tell me what's happening with you when it's happening, so I'm not surprised like that again."

"I love *you,* Julian, and I really am sorry. But if you're asking me to define myself for you . . ."

Ezri folded her arms, and took a deep breath. "I've got to figure out what I'm capable of, before I can share it with anyone else."

Julian shook his head, amazed, not sure he was hearing what he was hearing. Only a few days ago, they'd made plans to take a small vacation together, still three months away. "Ezri, are you telling me that you want to end our relationship?"

"No, of course not," she said, but he was suddenly sure that she was holding back. Her instant of hesitation, the shift of her brow, something.

"Well, is it that you feel like I'm limiting you?" He asked, starting to get confused.

"No. I'm—I just want you to let go, a little," she said, no longer angry, the soft plea in her voice even worse. "Let me decide some things. I want us to stay together, I just need to think about how things are changing, I need—I need you to be patient for a while. To give me some time."

He couldn't be mad at her for wanting his support, but he couldn't help being hurt by how she wanted it. Time alone, time away from developing their relationship, so that she could decide whether or not she wanted to develop it any further.

Are we back to kisses on the cheek? To close friends? What were the rules, the boundaries? Julian opened his mouth, not sure what he was going to say, amazed that the simple truth came out.

"I want you to be happy," he said truthfully.

It seemed to be the point, that keeping love meant maintaining a constant awareness that it couldn't be kept.

5

Nog was starting to really like Shar, so when he saw the Andorian sitting at the bar by himself, Nog eagerly joined him. Shar seemed to be just as happy about it, although Nog now knew his smile to be fake; he'd told Nog only yesterday about how humor and expressions of pleasure weren't big in Andorian society, that smiling was a learned behavior. Nog thought that was weird, but also entirely fascinating.

It felt good, to feel like Shar enjoyed his company. Nog knew that he was mostly well liked on the station, but his ability to make new friends had never been his strongest selling point. A lot of people in the universe looked down on Ferengi, for their mostly deserved reputation as a devious, swindling species, and it was nice to know that Andorians didn't appear to be one of them. It wasn't like hanging around with Jake, but Shar was so curious about everything, and he seemed to cast judgment on no one. It made spending time with him kind of fun.

It was early for dinner, and the restaurant was barely half full. They took a table next to the bar, Nog noticing that Frool seemed to be working alone when he stepped back up to order drinks and food. Shar had agreed to try a root beer.

"Frool, where's Uncle?"

Frool shrugged, turning to get the beers and mugs. "He keeps walking out in front for some reason, staring down the Promenade at something. This is the fourth time today."

"What's he staring at?"

"I don't know. It's down near the security office, whatever it is."

Nog turned and set the drinks down on the table, shaking his head. Uncle Quark had been strangely anxious ever since the attack, but not in a way that Nog would expect. If he was worried about another war, why hadn't Uncle liquidated any assets or sold any stocks, why hadn't he asked Nog to find him a new escape route? He seemed to be smiling too much, too, acting as though he was . . .

It hit him as he sat down, and he laughed out loud. Not anxious, *interested*.

"Why are you laughing, Nog?" Shar asked, his soft voice uncertain, as if he was afraid he'd missed a joke.

Nog leaned over the table, lowering his voice. "I think my uncle Quark might be in love."

Shar looked at him seriously. "His love is a source of humor?"

"The way he experiences it, definitely," Nog said. "I'm sorry, Shar, I was exaggerating. My uncle doesn't fall in love, exactly. It's more like . . . it's like he gets very excited about a possible temporary merger. He told me once that he knew he was in trouble every time he caught himself smiling for no good reason. That, or he buys flowers retail."

Shar tilted his head to one side, frowning. "He bought flowers for Lieutenant Ro."

"Really?" Nog laughed again, lifting his mug. "He's farther gone than I thought."

"You believe he wants to temporarily merge with Ro Laren," Shar said, and Nog actually choked. Sputtering, he put his drink down and shook his head at Shar, who was perfectly deadpan.

"That's *exactly* what I believe," Nog said, and Shar nodded. Nog had no idea if Shar had made a deliberate joke or not, but decided not to pursue the conversation any further; they were about to eat. The last thing he needed was to be thinking of his uncle Quark's romantic hopes for Ro Laren.

Shar tried the root beer, and liked it. As they waited for their food, Nog recounted a few of the minor adventures that he and Jake had gone through . . . although talking about his youth on the station reminded him of Jake's and his science-project field trip. It had been the first time Nog had ever seen a Jem'Hadar.

He finished his story about the self-sealing stem bolts and fell silent, unhappy that he couldn't seem to get away from thinking about *them.* He thought about Vic's advice, to find out what other people thought about the Jem'Hadar being on the station, but he and Shar had already talked about it. Unfortunately, the mild and pleasant Shar didn't seem to form strong opinions about much of anything. He had commiserated with Nog about his anger, but he hadn't expressed any of his own feelings, beyond saying that war was always unfortunate.

In fact . . .

"Shar, why don't you ever talk about yourself?" Nog asked. "It seems like you're always listening and asking a lot of questions, but you don't talk about what you like to do, things like that."

Shar blinked, his expression impassive. "I'm not sure what you mean."

"Well, do you have any hobbies? Things you enjoy?"

"I enjoy learning about different cultures."

Nog nodded; not dom-jot but it was a start, at least. "What's your culture like?" He asked.

Shar blinked again, and although his expression didn't change, Nog had a sudden impression that he was reluctant to answer.

"The Andorian culture is complex," Shar said, after a few beats. Then he fell silent again, as if considering how to proceed. Or maybe if he should at all. "Andorians have a genetic predisposition toward violent behavior, but socially, within our own communities, we're extremely structured. I would say we are a serious people, and adaptable. Compared to many other species, Andorians excel under difficult circumstances; like the human fight-or-flight response to danger, our biochemical reaction is to either fight or to increase our sensory input levels, which lends greater power to our analytical and reasoning skills."

So it *was* true. "That's very interesting."

Shar nodded. "All cultures are interesting," he said. "Your own, for example . . . you were telling me about your rules of monetary acquisition last night. Do all Ferengi know them, or just the males?"

Nog was deep into explaining the feminist revolution on Ferenginar before he realized that Shar had neatly sidestepped being asked any more personal questions. It was a common enough business tactic, a safe answer before turning the questions back on the customer, getting him to talk about himself. People loved to talk about themselves, there was a whole subset of rules on it. But why Shar felt he needed to divert him . . .

Maybe he's not all that thrilled about his roots, either. Nog was proud to be a Ferengi, but that didn't mean he was proud of everything the Ferengi people had ever done, and that definitely included plenty of his relatives. If Shar didn't want to talk about himself, that was fine by Nog.

Shar excused himself to get a drink he wanted Nog to try, and Nog sipped his root beer, his mind wandering. Thinking about troubled pasts, and wondering if Jake was having a good trip. He carefully avoided thinking about the station's uninvited visitor, or wondering what he would actually do if the Jem'Hadar's story was accepted as truth . . . and when Shar brought back two Andorian citrus drinks, Nog found that he had managed to keep himself in an optimistic mood. They both had hours of work to return to, hours of having to face the aftermath of tragedy in many of its dispiriting forms; a few minutes of not talking about how bad things were . . . well, that wasn't a bad thing.

Nog sipped from his new drink and thought he did a pretty good job of keeping a straight face, although the beverage tasted like a clear, fizzy version of a smell he'd once experienced, at an animal preserve on Earth. Goat, he thought it was called. In some kind of lemon oil.

Nog decided that they'd had enough cultural exchange for one day, reminding himself to discreetly ask Frool to clear the bar before bringing their meals. Maybe Shar wouldn't notice.

Quark tripped into the bar, imagining Ro's sweet breath in his ear once more. Only not threatening him this time, of course.

Well, maybe just a little, Quark thought dreamily, thinking of how she frowned when she was concentrating, that dangerous curl to her lips. Thank the River for transparent aluminum office fronts.

It was both exciting and disturbing, the way he was feeling, like an awestruck, passionate youth, like he was playing the market with his own money. Oh, there had been brief affairs over the years, what he believed to be mutually beneficial exchanges—no one had complained, anyway—but his serious infatuations were fewer and farther between than most people thought. He flirted with a lot of females, true, but actually thinking about them was a different kind of commitment altogether.

There had been Natima Lang back during the Occupation, and once briefly after the withdrawal, the first woman he'd purchased a gift for at retail. The Lady Grilka, now, *she* had been something; one of his closed deals, and he had the scars to prove it. There had been the magnificent Jadzia, of course, and by extension, Ezri—although his feelings were very different for the two incarnations of Dax. Ezri had a youthful quality that encouraged protective feelings, in addition to the occasional less-than-noble ones; but Jadzia . . . even getting shot down by Jadzia had been a pleasure, because she smiled and batted her lashes throughout, inspiring continued dreams of winning the lottery.

Ro Laren, now, she had Natima's passion, but Jadzia's sense of humor, she had Grilka's fire, plus a very appealing, haughty defensiveness that was all her own. She had a rebellious streak that could be profitable, considering her position. She was independent, headstrong, and antisocial, her inclinations didn't seem too expensive, and she had a shady past—not to mention, the kind of hands that men paid for. Ferengi men, anyway. She was exquisite.

To work on his growing mental file of her tastes and habits—research for expanding negotiations—he'd been randomly stepping out of the bar to observe her in her office. He noted what she was doing, collecting any information on her preferences that might work to his advantage. It was business, of a sort, but he was finding that it was a pleasure, as well. Her ironic smiles, her long legs, her habit of scowling to herself when she was deep in thought. Not only did he now know her preference for a hot beverage late in the day, information he could capitalize on, he'd had the extra enjoyment of watching her curse violently when she spilled it across her desk, leaping from her seat like a lithe but delicate jungle creature, mouthing words that would embarrass a Vicarian razorback wrangler.

Quark was snapped from his reverie when he realized that Nog and Shar were sitting next to the bar, eating. Love was something, but free labor was a lot harder to come by. Quark swept up to them, putting a big smile on for the Andorian's benefit. The boy had alerted them to a shrouded Jem'Hadar, after all, a talent too handy to frighten away . . . and he *was* a friend of Ro Laren's.

Quark had learned long ago that getting Nog to lend a hand was easiest to do with guilt, no raised voices or angry accusations, no threats. The fault was entirely Rom's, as usual, for refusing to discourage Nog's conscience when he was younger, but it was certainly too late to fix; anyway, until it stopped working, the guilt card saved the most time.

"Nog, Shar, how nice to see you," Quark said, turning his attention toward Nog, manufacturing a hopeful tone. "Say, Nephew . . . I know that you're busy making everything look nice for when the Federation shows up, but do you think you might take a look at replicator three for me while you're here? It's malfunctioning again, and I wouldn't ask except that I can't afford to hire anyone, not after the beating I took on your best friend's party yesterday."

Quark shifted his smile to Shar. "I probably lost thousands of strips in inventory alone, but Jake Sisko means so much to my nephew, I knew it was the right thing to do. I just couldn't turn away from family. Now that his father's gone, we only have each other."

Shar smiled back at him, his bright gray eyes sort of dazed. Andorians were a strange bunch, although Shar seemed mostly okay. He didn't gamble but he liked imported ale, which wasn't cheap.

Nog sighed dramatically, as if he'd been asked to shovel dung. "Uncle, my team has to rebuild the *De-*

fiant's venting conduit system tonight, *and* finish inspecting the lower core shield emitters."

Quark slumped his shoulders. "With all I do for you . . . that you could refuse me a scant moment of your time, just to offer an opinion on a simple replicator . . ."

Nog rolled his eyes, and Quark gave up. Threats rarely worked, but sometimes a flat demand did the trick. "Nog, just look at it, would you? I'm your *uncle*."

"Fine," Nog said, sighing again. "I'll look at it before I go back to work. Can we finish eating now?"

Finally. "You're too kind," Quark said, not working too hard to keep the sarcasm out of it. He turned to move back behind the bar, when Shar's combadge bleeped.

"Ensign ch'Thane, this is Ensign Selzner, in ops. You have a call waiting."

Selzner, the Starfleet communications officer with the overbite; she sounded very excited. Quark moved a few steps away but kept his head turned to catch the conversation, interested in what could make the intense, toothy Selzner sound like a teenager.

"Put it through," Shar said.

"It's straight from the offices of the Federation Council, on a directed channel," Selzner said. "And it's authorized for immediate uplink. Where do you want to take it?"

Quark forgot that he was pretending not to listen and turned, wide-eyed. Nog was also staring at the expressionless Shar, who answered calmly—but with a lifetime of experience staring into the faces of gamblers to back him up, Quark would have bet the bar that the Andorian was bluffing.

He's rattled, and he's not all that good at hiding it.

"I see. Would you send it to my quarters, please? I'll be there in five minutes."

"Ah, right. Affirmative."

Even as Selzner fumbled off, Quark was back at their table. "Why is someone at the Federation Council calling you, Ensign?"

Shar took a last drink from his glass and stood up, dabbing at the corners of his mouth with his napkin. Definitely anxious. "My . . . ah, mother works for the Council."

Quark nodded, starting to feel hopeful. "Oh, *really?* That's very interesting. What does she do? Secretarial work? Chef? Consultant?"

Shar shook his head, then smiled at Nog. "I apologize for having to leave, Nog, but I've been expecting this call . . ."

Thirishar ch'Thane, Andorians have . . . four distinct sexes, surname prefix denotes gender, 'Thane, that seems familiar . . .

Nog was standing up, too. "Hey, that's all right. I always take my father's calls, and—"

"Your mother is Charivretha zh'Thane?"

Quark blurted it out louder than he'd intended, amazed that this had slipped past him. A few arriving customers turned to look, to see Shar's obvious discomfort and Quark's elated shock. Zh'Thane held the Andorian seat in the Federation Council, very bright and very sharp, a woman who spoke her mind about everything. She was so influential, in fact, that her speeches and stands were often cited as vote-swingers, and thus influenced a vast number of possibilities—from election outcome pools all the way up to interplanetary resource contracts, the real big time.

This could bring whole new dimension to the concept of inside information . . . the blue kid science officer is zh'Thane's son.

Shar was already walking away, acting almost as if he was embarrassed that his mother was one of the Alpha Quadrant's top political figures. A big part of Beta, too.

He probably thinks people will treat him different, if they know. If they were smart, they would. Quark certainly planned to; the lovely Laren still pulled at his heart, not to mention his lobes, but Thirishar ch'Thane had his feet in the Great Material Continuum, and he probably didn't even know it.

Quark was definitely going to have to find out more about his nephew's new friend. The son of the Emissary, now the son of Charivretha zh'Thane; Nog apparently had an instinct for choosing powerful friends . . .

. . . and if he doesn't want to exploit it himself, why shouldn't somebody else benefit?

All this and the task force would be arriving soon, fresh blood for his dabo girls and many a merry Klingon getting roaring drunk on bloodwine. It seemed he'd been mistaken about something he'd said, only a day or two ago; the Federation really did care about the small-business man, after all.

The conversation went well until the very end.

Shar had expected the call, although he had

hoped that his *zhavey* would have remembered to contact him directly. Charivretha didn't fear the stain of nepotism, reminding him time and again that he had achieved everything on his own, but he knew that; it was the look on Nog's uncle's face that he'd been trying to avoid, a look that said he had changed in Quark's estimation because of his parentage. Shar wanted to be valued or ignored on his own merits, and now he would have to wonder; he had little doubt that the word was being passed along already.

Zhavey expressed concern over the attack and asked how his assignment was working out, listening with interest to his responses. By mutual agreement they didn't discuss politics, because there were too many facets of it that *Zhavey* couldn't talk about. They briefly touched on contacts with his other parents, leading up to what Shar had dreaded, to the inevitable topic of his future.

Shar listened calmly, looking into Charivretha's wide, lovely face, agreeing appropriately with tilts of his head. As his *zhavey,* she was his closest relative biologically and socially, and it shamed him to see the concern he had caused, the seeds of worry beginning to take root in *Zhavey*'s deep gray eyes.

Just as he thought he might get away without having to talk about it, Charivretha stopped her now byrote speech, gazing at him with love and the thing that he feared most, the threat of losing it.

"Thirishar, you are our only child. We didn't bear and raise you to have doubts about your obligations."

"No, *Zhavey.*"

"You are part of a whole. The covenant broken by one is lost by all."

"Yes, *Zhavey.*"

Zhavey studied him another moment, searching his face for something that didn't seem to be there.

"There's nothing for you to resolve," Charivretha said, and Shar couldn't disagree, he couldn't, not in the face of his *zhavey*'s unspoken anxiety—that he would disgrace all of them for the sake of his own selfish pursuits.

"I know, *Zhavey.*"

Zhavey looked away from him, and he could see the struggle for control. Charivretha zh'Thane was a person of great character and control, but she was also deeply unhappy.

Because of me.

"You'll call very soon," she half-asked, turning to look at him again.

"As is my duty and privilege, *Zhavey,*" Shar said, recognizing that she was letting him go, finished for now. It was both a relief and a sorrow. "Until then, I find you whole in my thoughts."

"As you are in mine."

The transmission ended and Shar's mind went blank for a moment, feeling something coming, his blood like a hot river crashing into his body.

With a low, primal hiss, Shar leapt to his feet and snapped a powerful kick at the logoed screen, boot heel cracking into the thick support post, the impact shuddering back through his body. The monitor burst into sparks, pieces of clear glass and dusky casing material shattering outward, clattering against the desk and floor. The fierce sense of triumph that accompanied his decisive action lasted only until he realized what he'd done.

Seconds later, when the computer asked if he needed assistance, Shar was able to answer in a mostly even tone, deeply remorseful and very much alone.

6

When Vedek Yevir finally called to tell her he was on his way to her office, Kira put the report she'd been reviewing aside and stood up, taking a couple of deep breaths. Ro Laren had kept the book, but Kira believed that Yevir should be told, to be prepared . . . and as a member of the Assembly, he would eventually be dealing with the book anyway, once Ro finished her investigation. Kira ignored the small voice at the back of her mind that told her she sought reassurance, that she desperately wanted to hear Yevir denounce the book.

Just because it hasn't been verified by some religious authority doesn't make it any less true, it doesn't change what's in the book. . . .

Ro Laren's voice, and it had a few other things to say, but Kira wasn't interested. Right or wrong, Ro had used up all her chances. One more challenge to Kira's authority, one more disrespectful outburst, and she could go find another job. And if Yevir wanted access to the heresy, Kira would see that he got it, however Ro felt about it.

She thought this just as the ops lift rose into view, Vedek Yevir standing tall on the platform. The quiet, unassuming man he'd been when he'd worked on the station had changed when the Prophets had reached him, through the Emissary . . . and Their gift to him had been a future in which he would undoubtedly someday be kai; Yevir Linjarin shone with the Prophets' light.

He'll know the book as false. He even said something about heresy at last night's service. . . .

Kira crossed her arms, frowning, watching Yevir step from the lift. It had been a moving service, well read and interpreted, and what he'd said at the end in his affirmations . . . something like, Reject all kinds of heresy, turn your back to unclean—

"Unclean words," Kira said absently, the framework of an unpleasant idea suddenly clicking into place. Her mind listed the pieces, bits of conversation and thought, fitting them together with the man who was walking toward her office.

He arrives only a few days after she was killed, to offer guidance.

The book is from B'hala.

She would have taken it to be recognized by a vedek, at the very least.

Turn our backs on unclean words. Reject heresy in all its forms.

It was a terrible thing to think, but now that she'd thought it, she was stuck with it—the possibility that Yevir knew about the book already, that he had known before he'd come to the station.

That he came here to find it.

Yevir reached the office door and smiled at Kira as it slid open, an honest, curious smile on his face.

"I'm sorry I didn't get back to you immediately," Yevir said, as they both moved toward the low couch at one side of her office. "I was talking with Ranjen Ela about a doctrinal difference currently being contested among members of the Assembly . . . Nerys, what is it?"

Kira sat down across from Yevir, deciding what she wanted to say. She was too distracted by the possibility of his deceit to talk about anything else, and wanted it cleared up.

So I embarrass myself. It won't be the first time.

"Vedek Yevir, were you aware that Istani Reyla brought an unverified prophetic artifact with her, to this station?" Kira asked, keeping her voice low, nonconfrontational.

Yevir wasn't a natural liar. He flushed, but held her gaze evenly and answered as though he'd been expecting the question. "Yes. It's one of the reasons I came. Have you found it?"

Kira nodded, taken aback by the admission, hoping he would continue talking, because suddenly she couldn't think of anything to say. His admission wasn't what she'd expected; Yevir was being discussed seriously as the next kai.

At her nod, Yevir became eager, his relief obvious. "Where is it? Has anyone read from it?"

Kira found her voice, but not to answer his questions. A vedek and a friend had lied to her, or at least withheld the truth.

"What's this all about, Linjarin? I think I have a right to know."

Yevir nodded slowly. "Of course. I should have told you already, but I was hoping that you would never find out about the book. I hoped I could find it and steal away, before anyone else was touched by its poison."

He smiled ruefully. "You must be angry with me, Nerys . . . and my only defense is that I wanted to avoid bringing attention to my search. The book is dangerous, and should have been destroyed millennia ago."

Thank the Prophets. She'd been right about the nature of the book. She thought she had convinced herself that the artifact wasn't credible, but hearing Yevir say it made her realize she'd been unsure, in spite of her declarations to the contrary. Whatever anger she felt toward him was more than made up for by the relief of finally knowing the truth.

"Tell me," she said quietly.

Yevir hesitated, then started to speak, his tone clear and direct. Again, it was obvious that he had given some thought to what he would say.

"The unnamed book has long been rumored to exist, through generations upon generations of the Vedek Assembly," Yevir said. "The story is that a man named Ohalu wrote it, a very sick and determined man, who plotted in his disease to sway people from the Prophets. He claimed that the Prophets spoke to him, and that they were a benevolent, symbiotic race of beings, learning from Bajorans just as we learn from them. He claimed that there was nothing sacred about them. Ohalu said that his truth would one day be recognized, because his prophecies would prove that he'd been contacted by the alien race."

Teacher Prophets, Kira remembered from the book, and shivered. She knew that a lot of non-Bajorans believed the Prophets to be an alien species. Even Benjamin, who had been Touched by them . . .

. . . but if the book isn't *a hoax . . .*

She'd read it, and been convinced that it was a fake because of how accurate the alleged prophecies were; skewed against faith and lacking any moral context, but factually correct. Kira felt an odd emptiness in the pit of her stomach, thinking about the prophecy of the Avatar.

"He managed to snare a few who'd lost their way with his sacrilegious views," Yevir continued, "forming a cult that existed to protect his heretical book, to keep it safe. They tried to promote their sickness, but the vedeks of that time put a stop to it. And that's where the story ends. The cult disappeared with the book.

"Once B'hala was discovered by the Emissary, the Assembly began to watch the digs for a number of things, Ohalu's book among them."

"To officially denounce it," Kira said slowly, wishing that she hadn't been so quick to give the book to Kasidy.

Yevir's eyes widened, and he shook his head. "To destroy it, Nerys. Don't you understand how dangerous it is? Istani Reyla read it, and brought it before the Assembly—and tried to convince us to turn the book over to the wife of the Emissary, saying that she should be told about one of the prophecies."

Oh, no.

"Prylar Istani was shouted down, but refused to surrender the artifact. She ran from the Assembly hall, surely driven to madness by whatever she found in that book. We have no idea what she planned to do with it, but if she could believe even a part of it . . ." Yevir shook his head. "The book destroyed her."

But I read it, too. Kira was shocked and concerned and confused, but she felt sane enough. For the moment.

"Where's the book now? How many have seen it?" Yevir asked, as Kira looked past his shoulder and saw both Kasidy and Ro at the door to her office, Ohalu's book in Ro's hands. Neither woman looked happy.

"My security officer found it during her investigation into Istani's murder," Kira said, no longer sure how she should feel about what was unfolding. All she could do was tell the truth now, as Yevir had done. "She and I both read it, and probably my science officer, who had it translated . . . and so did Kasidy Yates. I gave it to her."

"The Emissary's wife," Yevir said, his face pale. "We must pray, Nerys, that she's not infected."

Abruptly, Kira stood up, motioning for Ro and Kasidy to come in. It was time to straighten this out. The Allied task force was on the way, and there was too much work for her to do to continue wasting time on unnecessary etiquette. If everyone had been up-front in the first place, things wouldn't have gotten this far.

"As to where it is now, and what we're going to about it . . . Vedek, allow me to make introductions,"

Kira said. "I believe you've already met Kasidy Yates?"

There had been a match. The man who had stabbed the monk and then fallen to his death now had an identity, thanks to Bajor's Central Archives. Ro picked up the book and started for Kira's office, wanting to deliver the news personally.

Ro had just reached the ops lift on the Promenade when Kasidy Yates hurried to catch up to her, a padd in hand. Ro barely knew Captain Yates, but knew exactly what was on the padd; nothing else could account for the deep uneasiness on her face, the nervous tension in the set of her shoulders.

She must be on her way to see Kira, too.

They were the only two on the lift. Ro held the wrapped book tightly and nodded at Kasidy, not sure if she should say anything. She didn't want to be drawn into a conversation about the book before she had a chance to talk to Kira.

"Lieutenant Ro . . . is that it?" Kasidy asked, nodding at the book. Instead of the fearful hush Ro might have expected, Kasidy's voice was calm and clear.

"Yes," Ro said uncomfortably.

"May I ask why you're taking it to ops?"

Ro was still rummaging for a response when Kasidy shook her head. "Never mind. I suppose I'll know if I'm meant to know, isn't that one of the tenets?"

The tense, hostile tone wasn't directed at Ro, although she thought it was, at first, because the alternative seemed impossible; Kasidy was the Emissary's *wife.* Ro had heard that she wasn't a follower, but had never suspected such a depth of disdain for the faith.

A non-Bajoran, left alone to raise their baby, left alone to face a world of believers.

Now that she actually thought about it, Ro realized that Kasidy didn't have much cause to celebrate the Bajoran faith. Which made the prophecy even worse, the unfairness of Kasidy's situation making Ro wish she'd never found the damned thing.

"Captain Yates, I'm sorry," Ro said, sincerely meaning it. "If there's anything I can do . . ."

"It's Kasidy. And you can book me passage into another system," she said, and although she actually managed a faint, sarcastic smile, her tone was serious.

The lift opened into ops and they both stepped off, both walking toward the colonel's office. There were three Bajorans on shift, and Ro noticed that they each visibly brightened when they saw Kasidy. The wife of the Emissary either didn't see it or didn't care, her attention focused on Kira's office. Ro saw through the front window that Kira was talking to a vedek, and felt a conflict of emotions—disappointment, curiosity, and a kind of dark anticipation that she would want to think about, later. It was a childish response to the circumstances.

"That's Vedek Yevir, I think," Kasidy said, as they stopped on the platform outside her office.

The popular vote to be the next kai. Ro knew he was on board, but hadn't seen him yet. His back was to them, but from his hunched shoulders, he was definitely worried about whatever they were discussing.

And I wonder what that could be . . .

Kira stood up and waved them in. Kasidy immediately stepped to the door, Ro right behind her.

". . . allow me to make introductions," Kira was saying as the two women entered the office. "I believe you've already met Kasidy Yates?"

The Vedek stood up and faced them, nodding respectfully at Kasidy. "Of course. It's so nice to see you again, Captain."

Perfectly calm, except he didn't seem to want to look directly at Kasidy's face for more than a second. Ro realized from the flush beneath his tan that he was reacting the same way the other Bajorans had reacted, only more so.

It's like they think they're in the presence of royalty.

"This is Lieutenant Ro Laren, our new chief of security. Lieutenant, this is Vedek Yevir Linjarin."

She saw him glance quickly to her left ear, but he was discreet about it. "A pleasure, child."

Ro didn't answer, but Kira was already talking to Yevir again, her firm tone suggesting that she was following a course of action. Ro decided to see where she was going before she delivered the news.

"Lieutenant Ro appears to the holding Ohalu's book. Lieutenant, Kas . . . Vedek Yevir has just confirmed that the book was written by a dangerous heretic from the time before B'hala. The Vedek Assembly wants it destroyed, and considering the nature of the text, I'm inclined to agree with them—"

Ro started to protest, and Kira raised her voice slightly, talking over her, staring directly at Ro as she finished. "—to agree with them, because the members of the Vedek Assembly are the leaders of

Bajor's spiritual community, and this artifact falls under the scope of their authority."

Yevir was standing taller, reinforced by her blind trust. "Thank you, Nerys."

Kira ignored him. She looked between Kasidy and Ro, nodding at each. "As I said, that's my inclination. But I want to hear what you have to say about it . . ."

Her gaze sharpened on Ro, her expression sending a clear message—*I already know what you have to say. Stay in your territory.*

". . . because it's evidence in an inquest, and Kas, because the final prophecy concerns you directly. Lieutenant Ro, do you have anything new to report on your investigation?"

Ro nodded. There was no way to say it but to say it. "Yes. The bio results from the Archives just came in. The killer's real name is Gamon Vell. He was a vedek."

Ro had half expected to feel some satisfaction, telling Kira that one of her perfect religious leaders in her perfect religion had been responsible. But the shock in Kira's eyes, the look of betrayal behind it—

Ro had to look away, and she looked at Vedek Yevir . . . who didn't appear to be the least bit surprised by her revelation.

Yevir Linjarin felt great shame as the lieutenant revealed the truth, but reminded himself that he was right to feel shame. The Assembly had chosen an unwise path, and trying to cover for one's own responsibilities was not what the Prophets taught. And because he'd concealed the truth, the Emissary's wife had been exposed to lies and turmoil.

The faithless security officer stared at him. They all stared, and he accepted their anger and disbelief, taking it in and releasing it to the Prophets, accepting his own part. Best to tell it all, and bring an end to the matter as best he could.

"When Istani fled the Assembly, we knew she would come here," he said, taking a deep breath. He looked at Kasidy Sisko, praying that her distress wouldn't upset the Emissary's child, hoping that she would understand. "She believed in the prophecies, and wanted to show you part of the book. She said that you should know."

He turned to Kira, knowing that of all of them, she would understand best. Her belief was strong, her *pagh* untainted.

"By the time we decided we should try to intercept her, she was already on her way here," he said, looking into Kira's wide eyes, not shying from her feelings. "Gamon Vell, one of the strongest proponents of the idea, volunteered for the task, and left immediately. We didn't know that he was unbalanced, that his commitment to keeping this poison bottled would drive him to hurt her. There was never any intention to cause her harm, you must believe that, but we had to stop her from showing the prophecies to anyone else."

Kira's wounded gaze lay heavy in his heart. "I can't believe this," she said.

"Ohalu's book is like a spiritual disease, you surely know that," Yevir continued, not certain that Ro or Kasidy understood the gravity of what Istani had threatened, not like Kira. What he'd heard at the Assembly had been more than enough to convince him.

"Over thirty millennia ago, its influence polluted thousands of people, turning them away from the Prophets," Yevir said. "They were outcasts, pariahs, and still, they clung to their sickness of ego and fatalism. Through thousands of years, cults of this 'philosophy' rear up time and time again, like new strains of a virus, and that book—" He pointed at the bundle in Ro Laren's arms. "—is the source, the original flaw. It's dangerous, it teaches that the Prophets aren't deserving of Bajor's love, and we must stop it from infecting anyone else, no matter what the cost."

"Including Istani Reyla's *life?*" Kira asked, incredulous in her anger. "And the life of Gamon Vell?"

Yevir shook his head. "No, of course not . . . but don't you see, this only proves how treacherous Ohalu's prophecies are. If she hadn't been contaminated by the book, she wouldn't have run from the Assembly, and—"

"Are you trying to tell us that she caused her own death?" Ro Laren interrupted, speaking quickly, her tone heated. "That she *made* you send somebody after her, because she had a book that *offended* you?"

"Ro."

The warning in Kira's voice seemed only to fan the lieutenant's anger, but it also silenced her. She looked away, glaring, her head turned so that he could see her misplaced earring again. Yevir felt forgiveness in his heart for the hostile young woman, who so openly touted her inability to accept the Prophets. The book had probably only reinforced her estrangement.

"Excuse me," Kasidy said, her voice surprisingly mild for the depth of the anger in it, a thread of steel running through her demeanor that demanded attention. She dropped the padd she'd been holding to Kira's desk and crossed her arms, staring at Yevir as if he'd suddenly sprouted wings.

"Excuse me, but I read it. And I have to say, compared to some of what you consider to be *legitimate* prophetic writings, it's more accurate and a lot more complete. So maybe you're telling yourself that you're actually scared for the spiritual purity of Bajor, and maybe that's true . . . but maybe it's also true that the Vedek Assembly wouldn't look so good, if people knew about this book. Because that could mean that all those so-called heretics you've worked so hard to eradicate through the centuries . . . it could mean that you were wrong. That all along, you've persecuted people who had a justifiable belief system, just because it contradicted yours."

The security officer had reigned herself in on the surface, her tone angry but less accusatory. The viciousness came out in what she chose to say. "The suppression of a divergent religion, because its credibility is a threat to your own."

"It's wrong, but I don't know that I'd call lack of faith a religion," Kira said uncomfortably. "Lack of faith doesn't support any kind of spirituality."

Kasidy pulled her arms tighter. "Nerys, that's not exactly the point here."

"I wasn't trying to make a point. I'm just saying that the Bajoran faith is what has unified our planet. It defines us and our culture. It's what has carried us through our darkest times."

"Most of us," Ro said, almost under her breath.

Yevir felt cold to the marrow of his bones, seeing

their faces twist in fear and suspicion, the tension in their voices and bodies as their words sharpened.

"Don't you see?" he asked, raising his voice to be heard. "Look at how the book's sickness has already touched you, turning you from the face of the Prophets. What do you think would happen to Bajor?"

All three women fell silent, and for a few beats of his heart, he believed that they had finally grasped the nature of the disease—

—and then Kira, with a kind of furious determination about her that he'd never seen before, firmly pulled the book away from Ro Laren. She turned and thrust it at him, the book actually hitting his chest before he could fumble his hands into catching it.

"Nerys—" Yevir started, but she was already stalking from the room.

Ro and Kasidy both seemed shocked, and Yevir felt no less so. He thought he'd finally helped her to understand. Perhaps she felt torn between her spiritual and professional selves, which was a hard place to be . . . but he had faith in her. She had always turned to the Prophets for guidance.

She had given him the book, at least. Yevir was sorry for things that had happened, but the Prophets had surely sanctioned the end result: the Vedek Assembly had possession of the unnamed thing, and would deal with it appropriately. For the peace of the Bajoran people, and to the glory of the Prophets.

7

So, I think I'm a little confused. I haven't written in a while; it's almost as though I forgot how important it is, being able to talk to myself. There have been times that I've written pages of words, just to narrow my feelings down to a single sentence. I know my recent lack of interest is because I haven't wanted to talk to myself about Dad, but time is what I've got right now, time and a few questions I should already have asked.

I'm on the Venture, *drifting inside the wormhole. The sensors are a mess, not that I care much. It's funny, that now I find the time to think about what I'm doing a little more carefully. When I finally decided to do this, back at B'hala, I knew—absolutely—that I would stay for as long as it took, and that if I actually made it this far, I would spend every minute anticipating our reunion.*

Ah, naive youth. And hope. Because I wanted so bad to believe that he isn't gone, that these last few months have been just another adventure, another wild and seemingly desperate situation that all gets worked out in the end. Another situation that ends with my father and I, together, because I love him and I miss him in my life. When I translated the prophecy, it was an answer. A solution.

I've been here a single day, and with each hour that passes, my doubt flourishes. This is what I'm starting to think: The prophecy is an answer because I haven't been able to let him go. I was putting off the inevitable acceptance, and Istani Reyla showed up with a way out before I had to face my loss.

That's kind of a harsh summary, and not the whole truth. The prophecy itself, the parchment in my hand—there's power in it. It gives me a sense of the incredible, of the possible. . . . I'm not saying that the prophecy is false, just that my reasons for jumping right into it were certainly influenced by my hope.

Put like that, it seems too obvious. I've missed writing. I tell stories because I want to tell stories; I write because I want to understand.

The prophecy is real, I still believe that. I believe there's something genuine about it, anyway. But I also believe that if it isn't, if the whole thing turns out to be only madness and hope, I'll be okay. There's enough of me to take it.

I'll wait. Time is the one thing I have too much of.

8

Finished with her meditation, Kira opened her eyes and shifted position, from kneeling to sitting cross-legged. She reached out and extinguished the candle atop her *mandala,* feeling much clearer about the events of the day.

She sat on the floor of her darkened living area, thinking, feeling more relaxed than she had in a while. She'd decided that she would actually break for a late dinner rather than pop another ration pack in her office, to have a few moments at the small shrine in her quarters, and she was glad she'd made the effort. The updated ETA for the first Allied ships was less than ten hours from now, it wasn't as though she had a lot of time to spare, but a connection had been essential.

Because of what I've learned. Because of what I needed.

Ro, Yevir, Kasidy, the book, Reyla. Sustenance, faith was; although personal meditation wasn't as powerful as group, when she and her siblings all chanted their love together, there was nothing better for regaining a sense of guidance, of objectivity. In prayer, Kira was reminded that all would be well in Their eyes, as it ever was and ever would be. It also gave her a chance to step back and take account of her own thoughts and motives in everything that was happening, to review and improve, to try and understand other perspectives.

Kira smiled a little. She'd included a thought for Ro Laren in her meditation, which would probably really irritate the lieutenant if she knew. Someone like Ro couldn't seem to understand that faith and prayer didn't necessarily mean slavish devotion to ignorance. Ro exasperated her, but Kira couldn't help feeling sorry for her, too. If it was simply indifference she expressed, an apathy toward religion, no big deal. It was Ro's active anger at the faith that was distressing; something had driven her from the shrine, something that had made it a negative experience for her to trust in her own spirituality.

And as to Yevir . . .

She remembered Winn Adami too well to be surprised by duplicity within the Assembly, but Yevir didn't seem to be politically motivated; there was no question that he genuinely believed, and not for his own sake, but for Bajor's. It was the veracity of his love for Them that had clouded his judgment, and that passion had the potential to be too much for him, too much for anyone so deeply committed. To put such a man in a position of power could prove disastrous; people who believed in the righteousness of their every decision often stopped worrying about the consequences. The Prophets had faith in them all, but Kira was only mortal; she thought that Yevir's appointment to kai would be a mistake, and hoped that he wouldn't stay at the station much longer. With the task force and the Jem'Hadar and still, *still* the repairs, she didn't need to be worrying about how to interact with him at random intervals—

"Ops to Colonel Kira." It was Shar.

Back to the world. "Go ahead."

"The *U.S.S. Enterprise* has just popped out of warp. They've flashed a text message requesting docking clearance. requesting an immediate upper pylon docking clearance."

And so it begins.

Kira was on her feet, tapping at the closest light panel, looking for her boots. The *Enterprise* was the Federation flagship, but she hadn't expected anyone from the task force to arrive so soon, and she was surprised that they wanted to dock. Why hadn't they signaled hours ago? And a *text* message?

"Give them upper pylon two," she said, reaching for her uniform jacket.

"They report having suffered minimal but disabling damage from a plasma wave," Shar continued, "and list mid-level maintenance requirements in their request."

Plasma wave? The Badlands? That might explain their com troubles. "Status of DS9's senior officers?"

"Lieutenants Bowers and Nog are on the *Defiant,* working on the venting conduits. Dr. Bashir is in the infirmary . . . Lieutenant Ro is at the security office, and Lieutenant Dax is at cargo bay 41C, with the Jem'Hadar."

Kira could drag them all away from what they were doing, but she thought Captain Picard would understand if she greeted them by herself. She didn't want to wait, either, to find out how the *Enterprise* came to be docking for maintenance a full ten hours earlier than the fleet of "investigators" were expected.

"Inform Captain Picard that I'll be on hand to meet him personally, at the inner port, in ten minutes," she said. "Send two security guards to meet us there. And advise the *Enterprise* of our current supply and capacity status. Also adjust ETA for the Allied task force through them, as soon as possible."

She left her quarters immediately, smoothing her hair back as she walked, thinking about seeing Captain Picard and his fairly exceptional crew again; the *Enterprise*-E hadn't been to the station in some time, and despite the situation, she realized she was looking forward to it. Worf and Miles O'Brien had served with that crew, albeit on the *Enterprise*-D, and both men had some fascinating stories to tell. She knew that Ro had left the *Enterprise* to join the Maquis, another point of interest. The android Data was their science officer, and unless there'd been a change, Will Riker was the ship's second-in-command. Kira had only met Will once since her tragic run-in with Thomas Riker, and had been fascinated by the personality differences between the two. And Jean-Luc Picard . . . she remembered that she'd been a little intimidated by him, in a personal sense. He was formal, well educated, and well spoken, all qualities that tended to make her notice her own roughness.

But that was before I made colonel. Picard was sharp, too, and always spoke admiringly of Bajor. She wanted to know what he had to say about the Allied decision, and hear his opinion on Kitana'klan's story. In fact, the *Enterprise*'s counselor was a Betazoid, Deanne, or Deanna Troi . . . perhaps she'd be able to tell them more about the Jem'Hadar's motives.

She walked quickly through the Habitat Ring to the turbolift, wondering what else the *Enterprise* was about to bring to her entirely unprecedented day. At the moment, she felt like she couldn't possibly be surprised . . . and she knew from experience that feeling that way was usually when the universe decided to shake things up a little more, to try and find out what a person was created from, clay or sand, adapt or crumble.

As the lift started to rise, Kira thought she'd do best to keep her expectations to a minimum. Things were about to get hectic and she needed to keep her calm, to keep letting the Prophets lead, to keep knowing herself in the face of disorder so that she might lead others. All she could do was her best.

The station's air was cool and cleanly scented, the airlock room spotless, the lights lower than on the *Enterprise.* As much as Picard loved his ship, it was nice to set foot in less familiar territory every now and again. He wished the circumstances were different; the shock of seeing the debris field while approaching the station still hadn't worn off, nor the news from DS9's operations center that it was all that remained of the *Starship Aldebaran* and all who had been aboard her.

"Captain Picard," Kira said, stepping forward to shake his hand. Two Bajoran security guards were with her. The young colonel seemed tired, but calm, considering. "Welcome to DS9."

Captain Picard smiled politely, remembering her as the Bajoran intermediary under Sisko. Although they'd met before, most of what he knew about Kira Nerys had come from accounts of her actions during the war. She had been deeply involved in the Cardassian resistance against the Dominion, which by itself was impressive; Kira had grown up during the Cardassian occupation of her world.

"Colonel Kira, it's a pleasure to see you again," he said. "May I present Commander Elias Vaughn, on special assignment from Starfleet . . ."

Kira shook his hand as well. Vaughn smiled charmingly, but his eyes seemed to be studying the colonel's face intently. Kira smiled back at him. "A pleasure, Commander."

". . . and I believe you've already met my first officer, Commander William Riker."

Kira nodded, still smiling. "Of course. Hello, Commander."

"I'm sorry to hurry through the pleasantries, but my communications officer has just filled us in on your status, as well as news about the Allied task force," Picard said, "which I'm afraid is all news to us. We were hit by a wave in the Badlands, and haven't had the use of our subspace array for the last three days. We came here primarily for maintenance and repairs."

Kira nodded. "That explains it. I thought you were too early."

Riker stepped forward. "If I could get to a private room with a conference screen . . ."

"Of course," Kira said, nodding at one of the guards. "Sergeant, please escort the commander to the 3–3 conference room. It's the nearest."

As Will went to see what Starfleet had for them, Picard and Vaughn both expressed their sympathies. Kira accepted with grace, and explained their current shortages and deficiencies. Picard agreed to lend his chief engineer's services to Kira as soon as the *Enterprise* was pronounced fit, and the colonel offered ship leave for his crew, explaining that the Promenade was actually fully operational. As soon as the immediate plans were covered, the colonel brought them up to speed on the Allied response to the attack on the station.

"What's the word on establishing a peacekeeping presence in the Gamma Quadrant?" Vaughn asked.

"Ah, nothing new, that I've heard," Kira said, and Picard could see that she was surprised. He was, too; he'd assumed that Vaughn knew what was happening, but hadn't suspected that particular development himself. He supposed he should have; both the Romulans and the Klingons had wanted it when the treaty was being negotiated.

Although he shouldn't have said anything about it in front of me, or the colonel. And he seems positively enthusiastic about meeting her.

"If you haven't been in touch with the task force, you don't know about the Jem'Hadar soldier," Kira said. "I—excuse me, would you gentlemen like a drink, or dinner? And I'm sure your crew could use some station leave. Forgive my manners, I've had quite a day."

Vaughn accepted the offer for both of them. "The task force isn't going to get here any faster, no matter what we do," he said casually. "I think we can spare the time . . . although why don't we take a walk, instead? I've heard a lot about your station, I'd like to see some of it."

He looked at Picard. "That is, if you don't mind, Captain."

"Of course not," Picard said. "Although I hope you'll let me catch up to you in just a few moments. I need to make some arrangements with my senior staff."

"Of course, Captain. Would you care to see the Promenade, Commander?" Kira said. "We can walk the main floor."

"Elias, please," Vaughn said, following her away from the airlock. "Tell me about this Jem'Hadar."

It wasn't until after they left and Picard was back on the *Enterprise* bridge that it occurred to him—Vaughn had made no mention of the Orb, and neither had he. Entirely understandable, he supposed, given the circumstances. The news of the Jem'Hadar attack and the approaching task force had been quite a shock, and certainly overshadowed the far less galactic import of recovering the Orb of Memory.

After making arrangements with Counselor Troi to begin ship leave rotations, Picard found himself impatient for Will to report back, wanting to rejoin Vaughn and Kira quickly; he didn't want to miss Kira's reaction to learning about the Orb. After hearing about the *Aldebaran*, being part of something positive would do him good.

Ezri was just finishing the notes on her conversation with Kitana'klan when Kira signaled, asking her to come to the Promenade. It seemed the station had just received a visitor who knew something about Jem'Hadar development, and wanted to meet her.

Ezri hurried through the outer rings but found herself slowing when she reached the main floor, the turbolift exiting within sight of the infirmary. She stepped out and stood, looking at it, thinking.

She was a little worried about Julian, afraid that he'd been hurt by her desire to slow things down a little. It was strange, she actually had a memory of telling him that joined Trill tried to avoid serious romantic relationships, not long after she'd met him, as Jadzia. She'd only been half joking; although it wasn't discouraged in any way for the joined, it was widely accepted that other people could be a serious distraction from fulfilling personal potential—something else she already knew, but that she had only started to understand—

Julian walked out of the infirmary, adjusting his med kit on its strap. When he looked up and saw her, he barely hesitated, his expression moving from surprise to a kind of cordial ease as he approached. She knew him well enough to know better.

"Hello, Ezri." Polite, happy to see her, that unconscious stiffness in his manner. He made no move to touch her.

"Hi," she said, not sure what to do, standing with her arms at her sides. She wanted to reach out to him, to reassure him that they had time, that things would turn out for the best, but she didn't want to assume anything about what he was feeling. She'd asked for space and his patience, and he'd given it to her; it wouldn't be right to confuse things by trying to take care of him now, not when she was the cause of his discomfort.

Julian seemed to understand, and quickly said, "I'm on my way to see Kitana'klan, to replenish his ketracel-white. Didn't you see him today?"

"Just finished," she said, grateful for a safe topic. "He's the same, facts without interpretation, either won't or can't extrapolate meaning from environment . . . he maintains that Odo sent him to observe, and that he'll continue to cooperate with our restrictions until we're certain we can trust him."

"Where are you off to?" Julian asked. "It might be helpful for you to watch him interact with someone else. . . ."

"Actually, Kira asked me to meet her at the east platform. She says someone who just arrived with the *Enterprise* may be able to help shed some light on Kitana'klan. Maybe you should be coming with me."

"Can't," he said, smiling, looking into her eyes just long enough for her to be reminded of how beautiful his were, liquid and probing, always watching. "I don't want our guest to be suffering any withdrawal symptoms when I finally get there, thank you very much."

She smiled back him, and before she could find a way to end their conversation, Julian headed her off again.

"Well. I'd better get to it," he said. "See if Kira's acquaintance wouldn't mind stopping by the infirmary later, to fill me in."

"Sure," she said, and then he was gone, striding briskly away. Ezri took a deep breath, turned, and walked out onto the crowded main floor, reassuring herself that she'd made the right decision, for both of them. People changed all the time, and as much she loved him, she was going through a big transitional period. She didn't think she could focus on him as much as he wanted . . . and she was afraid that she might end up really hurting him. What had happened in her bedroom had been an accident, and maybe she hadn't handled it properly, but his reaction had been deeply painful to her; how would he react if something like that happened again? She wasn't human, and she didn't want to restrict herself by pretending that she was, just so Julian would feel more comfortable.

All of this proving that I'm spending too much time being distracted by him, by us, when I should be thinking about—

"Ezri!"

Ezri looked to the shout and there was Kira, standing with Jean-Luc Picard and . . . Elias Vaughn. *Vaughn,* of all people. Still alive. There was no mistaking him, even though he was obviously much older. She'd never expected to see him again. As she approached the trio, she randomly thought that at least she wasn't distracted anymore.

"Lieutenant Ezri Dax, Captain Jean-Luc Picard," Kira said, stepping back into a nook so that they weren't blocking foot traffic, "and Commander Elias

Vaughn. Lieutenant Dax is our counselor, and has been working with Kitana'klan."

Picard smiled, extending his hand. Jadzia had thought him attractive in spite of her feelings about him, and Ezri could see why. He had a strong presence, one that matched his finely chiseled features and the natural eloquence of his manner. "I believe I met a Dax when I was here last. And are you . . . I hope I'm phrasing this correctly—weren't you also Curzon Dax?"

"That's right," she said, noting that Elias didn't seem surprised at all. Either he knew already or he'd gotten even better at hiding his reactions.

Ezri felt a vague unease as she took Picard's hand; she knew that Benjamin had made his peace with it, and knew also that it hadn't been Picard's fault . . . but Locutus of Borg had been responsible for the death of Jennifer Sisko, Jake's mother and Benjamin's first wife. And both Curzon and Jadzia had been around to see what that had done to Ben, and to Jake. "It's good to see you again. Sir."

"Dax, it's been a while," Vaughn said, smiling. His hand was warm, his grip as firm as Curzon remembered.

"You're right, it has," Ezri said agreeably.

She suddenly realized Kira and Picard were both watching them.

"You two know each other?" Kira asked.

Ezri nodded, letting Vaughn respond. He was the one who'd brought it up, which meant he was obviously prepared to field questions.

"Long story," he said simply, and Ezri nodded again; worked for her. She thought he looked exceptionally good for a human who had to be around a hundred now, still handsome and full of life.

"It seems that Commander Vaughn has a wide knowledge of what Starfleet has collected on the Jem'Hadar," Kira said. "He was telling me about a new study on individual personality traits, when it occurred to me that you should be hearing this."

Ezri nodded, not bothering to point out that Starfleet hadn't done any such study, at least not officially; she'd spent the better part of two days reading everything she could find, starting with Starfleet's complete research. Included were outlines of results-pending hypotheses, and none of them involved psychological-sociological studies on individuality.

Vaughn will be Vaughn. . . .

Still the enigma, it seemed, although something had changed. He seemed taller, literally and figuratively, the literal coming from the fact that Ezri was easily Dax's shortest host. Julian thought it was funny, but changing stature made a huge difference in one's perception. It had always been strange, seeing the same people through different eyes, particularly when it had been more than a lifetime ago.

"It's easy to misjudge the Jem'Hadar," Vaughn said, off Kira's cue. "Because they're bred to fight and obey, most people assume that they're all alike, simplistic and solely driven by engineered instinct. In fact, it's coming to light that no two are the same. Their social status is partly based on it, on the strengths of individual character based on action and decision making. The most successful squad leaders are exceptional at reading the degrees of these qualities in their men."

"Is the status being considered as ascribed or achieved?" Ezri asked. The sociological equivalent of nature or nurture, and she was fascinated by the possibility that the Jem'Hadar were as complex as he was insinuating.

"Both," Vaughn said. "And there's a suggestion of personal evolution, especially among the older ones, of which there are understandably few. There's even a possibility that the need for ketracel-white decreases over time. It's still theory, but a series of autopsies on Jem'Hadar over the age of ten showed that some of them may actually have been producing a small amount of the enzyme. It's not consistent, or certain; the current thinking is that it's an age-related mutation, although it's also possible that there was simply a bad batch of genetic material around that time, and that the flaw has since been worked out."

Goran'agar, the one Julian tried to help on Bopak III, had been no younger than seven or eight. Julian was still firmly convinced that Goran'agar's freedom from the white had made him less violent. There'd also been Omet'iklan and Remata'klan . . . both of whom Jadzia had been able to observe up close. Both had seemed much more thoughtful and disciplined than the typical Jem'Hadar soldier. And both had shown signs, as had Goran'agar, of a nagging dissatisfaction with "the order of things." It was a sobering thought; if Vaughn's theory was correct, the longer a Jem'Hadar lived, the more likely he'd be able to overcome at least some of his genetic programming.

But Kitana'klan is barely three . . . if it's true that some older Jem'Hadar don't need ketracel-white, the Dominion would know about it . . . why would Odo pick such a young representative, if age actually matters?

"Have you dealt with any Jem'Hadar personally?" Kira asked.

"A few," Vaughn answered. "Enough to know that if your changeling friend actually chose this soldier for the reasons he gave, he wasn't chosen at random. Perhaps he represents the Jem'Hadar ideal. . . . Would it be possible for me to speak to him?"

Kira looked at Ezri, who nodded. It certainly couldn't hurt.

"Lieutenant, Commander Vaughn will be staying with us while he awaits his next assignment. Will you arrange quarters for him, and then take him to meet Kitana'klan?" Kira asked.

"Of course," Ezri said. "Captain, will you be joining us?"

Picard shook his head. "Actually, I was hoping you might show me to one of the station's Bajoran shrines," he said, addressing Kira, then glancing at Vaughn. "I understand an Orb is usually kept there."

"An excellent idea," Vaughn said, nodding at Picard before turning to Kira. "Colonel, I hope we'll be able to spend some time together later. I'd like very much to ask you some questions about the Bajoran faith, if you wouldn't mind talking to me about it."

"Not at all," Kira said, but Ezri thought she detected a slight edge to her voice, a stiffening of her smile. "I'd be happy to."

They split up, Ezri leading Vaughn toward the guest officers' quarters in the Habitat Ring. Strange, how small their corner of the universe actually seemed after a few hundred years. There did seem to be an inordinate number of recurring faces throughout Dax's experience, lending credibility to the idea that destiny or spirit decides who will be drawn to you.

Ezri wondered if they'd run into Julian somewhere along the way, and wondered, after eight lifetimes of love and loss and change, how it was that she could be missing him already.

Julian missed her already, but knew better than to let his focus wander as he reached Kitana'klan's cargo bay. The Jem'Hadar hadn't acted in a threatening manner yet, but Julian didn't want to take any chances. He asked both security guards on duty to accompany him inside, one to stay at the door and the other to stay with him; both would keep their phasers trained on Kitana'klan.

The soldier was standing in the far corner of the room. When he saw Bashir enter, he walked slowly to meet them, careful to be nonthreatening.

"Kitana'klan, I'm Dr. Bashir," he said, searching for something he could identify as emotion in the soldier's face, finding nothing. "We met yesterday for a few moments. I ran the physical scan."

"You were also at the table," Kitana'klan said. "With the Andorian who exposed me."

"That's right," Julian said, carefully and obviously reaching into his bag, his motions exaggerated. "I've brought you another white cartridge. I'd like to scan your metabolic fluctuations as you receive the enzyme, if that's all right with you."

"I have no objection," the soldier rumbled, still moving slowly as he knelt in front of Julian and the guard, Militia Sergeant Cryan. Devro was at the door. Julian prepped his tricorder as Cryan stepped around behind the kneeling Jem'Hadar, phaser ready.

Kitana'klan pulled the neck of his stiff clothing open, revealing a sputtering tube. Julian started to hand him a fresh cartridge as he ejected the old one, thinking that he might want to reset the numbers to account for stress factors—

—and then he was flying backward, and without his enhanced senses he might have missed what else was happening, it all happened so very fast.

Kitana'klan had grabbed the fresh cartridge and then dropped flat, pushing out and kicking at the same time, managing to knock both the guard and Julian down before rolling up into a crouch.

A phaser blast from Devro, at the door, high and outside, the scared corporal's hand skittering on the trigger—and the double *thunk* of white cartridges hitting flesh was impossibly fast, *thunk-thunk,* both hitting his right temple, the empty one not as loud, Devro falling—

—and only now was the pain registering, because Julian hadn't managed to save himself from hitting the ground in the two seconds that had elapsed, and because Kitana'klan was leaning over him, pulling at his upper chest, the pain immediate and wet, jagged bits of glass being dragged through his flesh, catching on muscle fiber too deep, too deep.

Julian pushed at the sneering monster with one hand, reaching for his combadge and not finding it, his heart pounding. His right shoulder was in agony and he was bleeding quite badly, his neck and upper chest hot and sticky-wet, the air metallic with the smell.

Kitana'klan hit him, a stunning punch to his temple, the blows that followed hazy and painful. At some point the soldier went away, and Julian opened his eyes. There was blood in them.

He concentrated; he had to diagnose the injuries before he could treat them. He felt weak and heavy, impossibly tired, his senses not gathering enough information. His right arm was losing sensation, and his right clavicle was surely broken, he could feel the crepitation. He'd lost a lot a blood.

Nicked subclavian, maybe. Two minutes perhaps before he bled out, if he could trust his own diagnosis.

Julian managed to roll his head to the side, and there was his med kit, less than a meter away. Harder to think, his mind wandering. There was a cauterizing seal patch in the kit, he always carried one. The patch would keep him alive for a few extra moments, assuming he hadn't suffered a hemothorax. Without a team standing by, a breach of the pleural cavity meant he would certainly die.

Julian wanted to reach for the kit but then it was gone, kicked away by the boots that walked past his flickering gaze. He thought that he should at least apply pressure to the wound, but couldn't feel either hand anymore. Didn't matter, he'd just bleed out internally. . . .

Blood was splashing and getting darker, ebbing

away into the encroaching swarm of blackness. His brain was starving; he'd lose consciousness and then die. The thought seemed uninteresting and distant . . . except he wished he had seen Ezri one last time, the thought of her face making him sad, and he thought of Kukalaka, his stuffed toy from childhood, and then he thought nothing at all.

9

Kira found that Picard was a lot less intimidating than she'd remembered, although it probably had a lot to do with the respect he showed to Vedek Capril, and to the Orb itself. The Orb of Contemplation was now in a private room that adjoined the shrine, and Captain Picard had asked to see it in a truly reverent tone, confessing an interest in Bajoran artifacts.

Vedek Capril left them alone and Kira watched as Picard walked in a circle around the supported ark, hands behind his back as he leaned in closely, examining the carved detail. She knew he'd seen it before, but wouldn't have guessed from looking at his face; his gaze was very bright, the slight smile he wore a genuine expression of wonder. His few questions indicated that he knew as much about where and when the Orbs had been found as most Bajorans.

When he finished his scrutiny of the ark, he stood straight and adjusted his uniform, still smiling.

"Colonel, it's seems to be a matter of fate that the *Enterprise* comes to be at your station."

Kira nodded, a little puzzled at his choice of words. Picard's ship needed repairs and access to subspace communications; she wasn't sure that qualified. *Probably means to meet with the task force.*

"May I arrange to have something beamed directly to our position from the *Enterprise?*" Picard asked, looking at the ark again, obviously fascinated by it. "It was actually Commander Vaughn's discovery, but I think he expects me to present it. Kind of a surprise gift, to go along with our surprise visit."

He looked at Kira again on the last, and she had the impression that beneath his pleasantly placid exterior, he was grinning. His eyes sparkled with good humor.

"Of course, Captain," she said, feeling slightly apprehensive.

Picard gave their coordinates to someone on his ship, and a few seconds later, a small object materialized at their feet. Kira couldn't credit what she saw for a few blinks, thinking that she'd somehow misseen it, but it didn't waver. It was an ark for a Tear of the Prophets.

"We believe it's the Orb of Memory," Picard said as Kira moved toward it, reaching out to touch it, knowing that it *was* the Orb of Memory as a sigh escaped her. The design at the opening was a series of curved lines radiating out from a central sphere, a design that every Bajoran child knew as belonging to the missing Orb.

She was speechless for a moment, so struck with awe that she forgot Picard was present. The mystical, beautiful connection to the Prophets that each Orb represented was always cause for joy, but to see one that had been taken away early in the Occupation, lost to Bajor for so many years . . . to know that it was with them again was a blessed, precious knowledge, and for just a few seconds, it filled her up.

"Where did you find it?" Kira asked finally, unable to take her hand from the closed ark.

"In the Badlands, actually," Picard said. "On a derelict. Commander Vaughn led the away team, so I'm sure he can better describe the exact circumstances."

Kira straightened, the depth of her gratitude and happiness inexpressible as she turned to Picard. She floundered for an appropriately diplomatic response to his miraculous gift, aware that words were insufficient but that they were all she had.

"Captain, on behalf of the Bajoran people, please allow me to thank you and your crew for what you've done."

Picard nodded, a deeply satisfied look on his face. "You're welcome, Colonel. I have some idea of what this means to Bajor, and I'm delighted to have played even a small part in returning it to you . . . though it really is Commander Vaughn you should be thanking."

"I will," Kira said, gazing at the Orb, deciding who she should contact first, thrilled to have such a decision to make. Shakaar was still on Earth, she thought, but that might be the best—

Her combadge signaled, and her bright mood immediately darkened. She stepped away from Picard and the beautiful ark, expecting the call to be trouble; she couldn't imagine the day bringing anything else at this point, and although she'd planned to keep her expectations to a minimum, it was turning out that she couldn't expect her plans to work out, either. . . .

Keep it together, you haven't slept in at least twenty-six hours.

"This is Kira."

"Colonel, this is Ro," Ro said, sounding out of breath. "I've got a situation here with Vedek Yevir, and Kasidy Yates is also present, and I, ah, *request* your immediate presence at the security office. Sir."

Not just out of breath. Ro sounded like she was about to kill someone.

"On my way," Kira said, looking back at Picard as she tapped out. Ro's office was close, but she didn't want to leave the Orb unattended, and it didn't sound like she had time to track down Vedek Capril, he'd been on his way home . . .

. . . *the candle cabinet.* There was an indiscreet panel on the south wall of the small room, a space where extra candles were stored. The shrine was closed for the evening, but she wanted to take the extra precaution, at least until she had time to tell one of the vedeks about it.

Perhaps after Yevir leaves . . . An unkind thought, but sincere. She wasn't feeling particularly trusting toward her old friend's motives.

"My apologies, Captain," Kira said, "but I'm needed somewhere immediately. Would you mind terribly if we put off announcing the Orb's return for the moment?"

Picard smiled, shaking his head. "The Orb belongs to you now. And I should be returning to my ship, to prepare my own argument against what the

Allies have in mind. I'm sure you've got enough to do without having to escort me around."

Kira asked Picard to open the cabinet for her, and she gently lifted the ark, putting it on a low shelf. It would be safe. The Prophets had wanted it brought back to Bajor, or it wouldn't be here.

Kira suggested that they walk together toward the security office; there was a turbolift directly across from it. Picard nodded, and they walked out onto the Promenade, Kira just putting one foot in front of another, moving toward the next event in line. The Prophets knew that she rejoiced inside for the return of the Orb, but she had the station to consider, and the idea that Ro might stab Vedek Yevir with something had to take precedence over her own elation.

Things were bad, and they were probably going to get worse. When she realized that there was no point in trying to tell Yevir anything, Ro called Kira and then held her tongue, letting the man quietly poison the air. Kasidy had arrived only a few moments after the vedek and had watched their exchange silently, her arms crossed, her face drawn. When he'd started his monologue, she'd turned away.

Hurry up, Kira, Ro thought miserably, fighting an urge to leave the office and an even stronger one to start yelling. Yevir was exactly the kind of man she most disliked, so convinced he was right that he believed the entire universe was backing him up.

"—worse than malicious, it was immoral and criminal," Yevir was saying, calm and absolutely furious, his polite words dripping with threat. "I'll see to your immediate dismissal, and that you're remanded to the custody of the Militia's justice department. I can only hope that you'll find the love of the Prophets in the end, to beg their forgiveness for what you've done . . ."

Where is she? Ro looked past Yevir, and—

—oh.

Yevir was still talking, but Ro didn't hear him. Standing not two meters in front of her office was Jean-Luc Picard. Kira was with him, but that didn't seem as important, *I knew a starship had docked but not yours . . .*

Picard, who had once trusted her because she'd given her word. Ro hadn't seen him since she'd broken it, but had spent many a moment in the years that followed wishing that things had been different. Regardless of the necessity of her actions, she knew she'd disappointed him, and being a disappointment to Captain Picard had easily been the worst consequence of her decision. The intensity of her feelings seemed too obvious, her own father had died badly when she'd been a child, but Ro wasn't sure what it was; she'd just always wanted his respect.

The captain looked past Kira, glanced at Ro—and quickly found her gaze, his own as sharp as blades as he studied her, frowning. Yevir was still telling her how much trouble she was in, and Kira had turned away from Picard, heading for the office door, but Ro was frozen, feeling herself flush with shame, hoping it wasn't showing. How many years had it been? Long enough for her to have forgotten what a hard place it was to be, standing in the path of his scrutiny, *knowing that you're being inspected and are about to be found wanting—*

Picard held her gaze a second longer and then turned his back to her, walking to the turbolift. He didn't look at her again.

Great, her defenses mustered, laying on the sarcasm. *This is just wonderful, a real experience. I needed a reminder that I don't belong anywhere, that I don't measure up. . . .*

Kira stepped into the office and Yevir immediately turned his attention to her, demanding that Ro be dismissed, that she be disciplined severely. Poor Kasidy looked as though she wanted to be physically ill.

Kira didn't even look at Yevir, fixing her gaze instead on Ro, completely ignoring the vedek's apoplexy. "Report, Lieutenant."

"Colonel, it appears that approximately three and a half hours ago someone with access to the translation of Istani's book uploaded it, in its entirety, into the Bajoran comnet. Reports are being filed to the station from every province, asking about it."

Kasidy finally spoke, looking at Kira pleadingly. "I just got a call from the Commerce Ministry; they want to know if they can issue a release saying that I believe the prophecies are false. They said they've received over a thousand direct calls in the last hour from people asking to speak to me."

Kasidy lowered her voice, but Ro could hear her. "Nerys, I don't want to deal with this, not now."

Kira took Kasidy's hand and squeezed it, looking into her eyes. "Everything is going to be okay, Kas."

"I don't see how you can say that," Yevir said, still managing to keep his voice down, still playing the part of the angry victim. Maybe he actually felt that way. Ro figured it didn't make much difference, in the end; he was a fanatic.

"All moral issues aside, a crisis has been deliberately unleashed, and all because an admitted opponent of the Vedek Assembly was given access to sensitive materials," Yevir said. "She used her position to promote her own intolerance, with no thought as to how it would affect anyone else."

He was glaring at Ro as he spoke, and she decided that she was ready to end this particular party, hopefully with Yevir's apology. Seeing Picard had left her off balance, but she was still confident that Colonel Kira would believe her word over Yevir's. Ro knew she didn't come off that well with a lot of people, but even her enemies knew her to be honest, and she had never lied to Kira about anything.

"Colonel, I absolutely did not," Ro said. "Vedek Yevir is mistaken. I haven't seen the translation or the book since we all met in your office this afternoon, and I had nothing to do with its transmission to Bajor's communications network."

Yevir smiled, a small, sanctimonious smile. "The word of a nonbeliever, that certainly holds its own with a lie."

"Please don't call me a liar," Ro said, just tired of listening to him.

"I didn't, child, I just don't understand why you won't admit to it," Yevir said. "You're the only one here with reason. That treacherous book validated your damaged beliefs, and you couldn't stand to be alone anymore, could you? A nonbeliever from a world that embraces spirituality—"

Kira was nodding along, her expression neutral.

When he hesitated long enough to draw breath, she spoke quickly, looking directly at Yevir for the first time.

"I did it," Kira said. "I uploaded Ohalu's book."

Yevir finally shut his mouth, but Ro felt her own hanging open.

Kasidy didn't believe her. They all stared at her, and Kas saw her own feelings in their faces—Ro's eyes were wide with incredulity, and Vedek Yevir looked like he'd had the wind knocked out of him.

"You're joking," Yevir said. He seemed smaller, somehow.

Kira's chin was raised, her head high. "I gave a lot of thought to what you said earlier. You asked me what I thought would happen to Bajor if the book were made public, and after I considered it carefully, I came to the realization that you don't know the Bajor I know."

Yevir was the very picture of injured confusion. "Nerys, I don't know what you're talking about."

"The Bajoran people aren't children," Kira said. "They don't need anyone to censor information on their behalf, and frankly, Vedek, I'm surprised and a little offended by the Assembly's attempt to do so. It's patronizing, it suggests that you don't think the Bajoran faith is strong enough to tolerate a different perspective."

"And this is your answer?" Yevir asked. "To send blasphemous and offensive words into people's homes, like some kind of . . . of *test?*"

Kira didn't hesitate, her manner angry but controlled. "And are you that desperately afraid that they'll fail? I'm tired of wondering whether or not I'm being manipulated by people who say they speak for the Prophets. I have my own relationship with Them, and I trust my own judgment. And whatever you think about that, what gives you the right to decide what's bad for me, or what's best for anyone besides yourself?

"I see it as an opportunity for all of us. Here it is, almost eight years since the Occupation ended, and we still haven't found our balance. I see our world as a place that's trapped in transition. I see a struggle to integrate the cultural spirituality of thousands of years with what we've learned in the last century, and I think a good look at ourselves is exactly what we need to get through it, to create an atmosphere of positive change. To let every Bajoran reevaluate what the Prophets mean for their lives."

Yevir was aghast. He ran one hand through his silvering hair, mussing it, his face screwed up in distress as he took a half step back.

He's not faking it, he really thinks this is a holocaust. Kas could understand his reaction, could see perfectly why he felt so betrayed. And she could see why Kira might have done it; the politics couldn't be plainer. The thing was, Kas still didn't actually believe it.

"I love the Prophets," Kira said seriously, still addressing Yevir. "And it doesn't matter to me what anyone thinks of my faith, because I know the truth. Reading that book only confirms for me that the love of the Prophets can be interpreted in other ways. I prayed about this, and I truly believe it's the right thing for Bajor. I've been given a sign, that the

Prophets support us. Ohalu's book belongs to every Bajoran, Vedek; please, have faith in *us,* have faith that each individual can only grow as the Prophets intend."

Ro seemed almost to smile, and for some reason, that look of approval finally did it for Kasidy's belief problem. Kira Nerys, who had been there for her, who had helped her find workers and apply for permits on her new home, who had been a real *friend* to her . . . Kira Nerys had just created absolute chaos for her and the baby. And she had done it on purpose.

Kasidy hated public confrontation, but there was no help for it, she needed to understand and she needed it *now.*

"How could you do this to me, Nerys?" Kas asked, and Kira turned away from Yevir, finally, her head not quite as high. She at least had the decency to look ashamed, but at the moment, Kas didn't care a whit for Kira's shame. What good did it do her?

"Kas, I'm so sorry," she said, and it certainly looked like she meant it. "It was just—it was the right thing to do, I had to do it."

"That's fine, good for you," Kasidy said tightly, folding her arms, and then she took a deep breath, *baby, it's okay, relax,* then another. The kind of anger she was feeling couldn't possibly be harmless. After another deep breath, she started again.

"So you and the Vedek Assembly have now each made a grand statement of how right you are," Kasidy said, making the anger and pain become words instead of heat, struggling to keep her body from reacting to her distress. "I can appreciate that. But I didn't ask how you could do this, I asked how you could do this to *me.* To be honest, I don't care why, because all of this means that if I want a moment's peace for the rest of my pregnancy, I'll have to go into hiding."

Silently watching her, Kira was obviously unhappy, her expression guilty and apologetic—which for some reason seemed to make things worse. How convenient for Nerys, that she could betray her friend and then feel sorry about it, knowing all the while exactly what she was doing. Kas knew she wasn't being entirely fair, but decided that she was allowed.

She looked at Yevir, at the way he was practically wringing his hands, his thoughts as clear as if they were written in the air above his head, *The mother of the Emissary's child's is unhappy, oh, dear, what can I do?*

Relax. Breathe.

"I'm sorry, but this is not okay," Kas said slowly, talking to herself as much as to Kira and Yevir, her words gathering speed as they poured out. "I can't stay here if this is what it's going to be like. I'm a person with a *life,* I'm not some indirect religious figure in a cause, and if you think I'm going to let my child be involved in any part of this particular dilemma, think again. Ten thousand Bajorans, dying so that my baby will be born into peace, so that he or she can be worshiped as some kind of spiritual embodiment, as some *thing?*"

Kas folded her arms tighter and then deliberately relaxed them, so tuned to the second life inside her that she almost reflexively protected it now. It wasn't a matter of choice, her current priorities didn't allow for choice; she just couldn't have this in her life.

"I'll leave," she said calmly. "I'll get as far away from here as possible. In fact, my things are already packed."

I could *leave.* It sounded so possible, so easy. So tempting. *Just . . . fly away, and never come back.*

Her pronouncement was followed by silence. All three of the Bajorans in the room looked mortified, but as far as Kasidy was concerned, Ro was the only one with any credibility, the only one who hadn't actually done anything wrong.

Before anyone could speak, a man's unfamiliar voice spilled out of an open com on Ro's desk, deep and clear and very fast.

"Security alert, the Jem'Hadar soldier has killed at least two people and is no longer in containment. Starfleet medical officer down, needs emergency transport to medical facilities, Dax is with him. We're at cargo bay 41C or C41, this is Commander Elias Vaughn, acknowledge."

Kira hit her combadge as the last words were spoken, calling for medical transport, already striding for the door; Kasidy barely had time to get out of her way. Ro acknowledged and hit the security alert, and Yevir Linjarin stood uncertainly, perhaps wondering who he would complain to now.

Worried and wounded and afraid, Kas left immediately for her quarters, planning to throw the manual on her door as soon as she got there. No matter what else happened, she was moving away from DS9 as soon as possible.

10

A monster, looming. Troubled sleep, and pain. Someone calling his name. A bone-deep *ache,* so pervasive that his own body was a stranger to him, numbed flesh warming up just enough to scream at the cold, cold air.

But I'm dead.

It was Julian's first whole thought in a while, and the paradox exhausted him. Kitana'klan had killed him, but he couldn't remember dying so he couldn't be dead. The pain was terrible, it made his next breath into a cry for relief that emerged as a helpless whimper.

That tiny sound of pain and he was *with* the pain, the sound bringing him closer to full consciousness as it defined him from the dark. He couldn't think, the level of awareness too much, the totality of the pain making him afraid that he might lose himself—

—and then Ezri was there, talking softly, explaining that he'd been hurt and that they were going to the infirmary. He couldn't see her, didn't know if she was touching him, but her voice was enough. It was clear and firm and she told him that she loved him. Julian fell asleep before she finished, but he wasn't afraid.

Vaughn should have called the alert as soon as he saw that there were no guards posted outside the bay. Neither he nor Dax carried a weapon, and if there was a situation inside with the soldier Kitana'klan, going in unarmed meant no chance. As opposed to a slim one.

His instincts telling him that the Jem'Hadar had escaped, Vaughn didn't bother to think about procedure. With a curt nod from Dax, they walked through the unlocked door, Vaughn in the lead.

He took in as much as he could as soon as they were inside, wasting no input that could help his assessment. Smells of scorched material and blood, phaser fire, exposed insulation. There was a splash of blood on the inside of the door, and a trailed smudge leading to the first body, a Bajoran militia corporal, young, probably human. Throat cut deeply after the body was moved, from the pool of it he lay in now.

Another young man at eleven o'clock some distance away, Starfleet medical, still alive but in bad shape, deep claw marks seeping across his chest, a cauterizing pack at the base of his throat. There was a med kit close by, adrift in the doctor's blood.

Bajoran Militia sergeant, the third victim, not far from the doctor. Another kid, his head twisted around at an angle that counted him dead.

Within a few seconds, Vaughn had all the information he needed to get things going. He stepped back to the door and hit the companel as Dax ran to the survivor, snatching up the bloody med kit before crouching next to him.

Vaughn relayed the prioritized facts quickly, spotting a dropped tricorder on the floor as Dax and the wounded doctor sparkled away to a medical facility. A Lieutenant Ro acknowledged, telling him to secure the situation as best he could, that security and Colonel Kira were on their way.

DS9 had underestimated the soldier, but it hadn't been their fault. In the war, the Allied troops had mostly faced off against soldiers only weeks old, deadly but untrained, unfocused.

A Jem'Hadar who'd had extended training for hand-to-hand and small arms wasn't nearly so easy to kill as a violently impulsive youth, however. The Jem'Hadar got faster and better at everything with practice, so even at a year or two of age, depending on how often they used their skills, the studied soldiers were effectively unbeatable without weapons. Their reflexes were simply better than those of most humanoids.

Obviously, there were species who could hold their own physically against the Jem'Hadar—Klingons, for example. But whereas Klingons' code of honor could make them respect, even admire an enemy, the Jem'Hadar were bred to see every opponent as inferior; no respect, no mercy, and for a Jem'Hadar, victory was life. They weren't interested in glory or lasting honor, just the win. How they got it didn't figure into the equation, and that made them extraordinarily good at killing.

As soon as he'd signed off, Vaughn ran to the tricorder and scooped it up, setting the readings with one eye while he searched for a phaser. The Jem'Hadar soldier certainly had one of them, but perhaps not both—

—*there,* near a stack of empty boxes by the door. Vaughn paused in the tricorder adjustment long enough to grab it, the sharper sounds of his movement resounding through the cool air of the dead and empty bay. Only seconds later, the station went to red alert, a light panel on the bay wall starting to flash, a distant alarm sounding.

Vaughn ignored it, working on the tricorder. A shrouded Jem'Hadar standing still could be detected easily enough, almost all energy was observable, but to track one you had to be exact, *and better at running science equipment than I am, dammit, what's the formula*... Vaughn knew a lot of theory, but rarely had to practice.

As with a ship's cloak, gravitons were produced by a Jem'Hadar shroud aura. There was a way to pattern the residue, to follow it, but the trail dissipated quickly. Vaughn assumed that Kira would want to track Kitana'klan from ops, but he'd also gathered that the station's internal sensors weren't a hundred percent, and he knew that a full sweep on a station the size of DS9 would take time. It was unlikely that the sensors could even pick up such a delicate trace; from the reports Vaughn had read about the process, a tricorder was definitely the tool for the job. If he could follow the soldier for long enough to narrow the search perimeter even a little, it could make a big difference.

He was just finishing with the tricorder when the

colonel walked through the door, followed only seconds later by a Bajoran security lieutenant and five noncom guards, all of them armed. Good. He didn't mind the idea of having an escort; it was highly unlikely that the Jem'Hadar wanted to be followed, and the more of them, the less likely he was to attack.

Vaughn rapidly outlined the residue-pattern theory, explaining that he'd never tried it firsthand. Kira liked it, recommending that they coordinate the effort with ops, letting the station's sensors take over when they picked up a definite direction. She put a call in, absolutely on top of things, not looking at the two dead boys but not looking away, either. Vaughn was impressed.

One of the Militia guards volunteered that she'd worked as a sensor array tech and operator. Vaughn gladly turned the tricorder over to her and waited for Kira to finish her instruction to a science officer named Shar, in ops. Vaughn assumed it was zh'Thane's child, Thirishar; he'd accessed DS9's current personnel files before the *Enterprise* had docked, gaining all sorts of highly classified insight into some of the people on the station.

"Colonel, I'd like to apprise Captain Picard of this situation," Vaughn said, as soon as Kira tapped out. "And ask him to stand by to assist."

"Please," Kira said. "And tell him I'm open to suggestions on how to resolve this thing before it goes any further."

The tech/guard held the tricorder up, motioning at the door. "I've got it."

They fell in around her, Kira and the tech taking the lead, Vaughn hanging back to talk to Picard. As he filled the captain in, he found he couldn't stop staring at the dead corporal's open eyes, his clawed throat, the fan of thickening blood on his forehead from a pair of deep cuts. He looked surprised, caught off guard by the end of his life. He looked dead.

If they didn't find and stop the Jem'Hadar ASAP, a lot more people were going to end up the same way. Vaughn could think of a dozen ways that one determined person could destroy a space station without too much trouble, and that was without being invisible . . . or a Jem'Hadar soldier, who was always willing to die if it meant he could take out his enemy in the process. To them, death meant nothing, but it was a victory if they didn't go down alone.

Five minutes. If they didn't have a clear idea of Kitana'klan's intent by then, Vaughn was going to start pushing for a full evacuation. They couldn't afford anything less.

Ezri acted unprofessionally. She didn't reflect or consider. As soon as she stepped into the bay behind Vaughn, she saw Julian. And there was so much blood, what seemed like bucketfuls splashed across his face and chest, puddles of it all around him, that she knew he was dead. Knew it. And that was when she saw his chest rise, and when she took action.

Not thinking about the possible dangers, not thinking about anything but how important he was, how she had to make him stay with her, Ezri ran to him, grabbing the med kit off the bloody floor before dropping to his side.

He was so pale, the blood seemed ludicrously

bright against his skin. His tattered jacket and the shirt underneath were soaked with it, but the gashes on his chest were only oozing. The seal patch on his collarbone might have stopped the major bleeding, she didn't know, and she didn't want to make anything worse by jumping to medical assumptions—

"Julian, can you hear me? Julian?" Ezri asked, not expecting a response, wondering why they weren't already at the infirmary—and he let out a semiconscious moan, so soft that she barely heard it.

He winced, his mouth twisted, an expression of hopeless suffering, and Ezri started talking, reassuring him. Comforting him. She took his hand, noting with alarm that his fingers were scarcely warmer than her own, keeping the alarm from her voice; she told him that she loved him, and that he would be all right.

She was looking at his blood-spattered face as the environment around them changed, as they were transported to an emergency table, flush with the floor on one side of the infirmary's operating theater. Ezri quickly stumbled away and someone touched a command, the section of floor rising, Julian's devastated body rising up to meet the waiting, healing hands of Dr. Girani. He wasn't conscious, and his eyes were partly open, and Ezri didn't know if he would live.

Ezri called up her memories, Dax's memories, searching for an appropriate response to her fears, some relief, something she could *do* . . . and couldn't find one. Dealing with life and death on an emotional level was one of the very few things that all hosts had handled in their own way, because the feelings were so complex, so intimate, so specifically tied to each relationship. There was no simple concept to grasp, nothing from their past that could help her.

So, I'll deal with this as Ezri, she thought, and as she thought it, she realized what she wanted. It wasn't a choice from fear, although she was afraid . . . it was that she just knew now, it had hit her and she couldn't deny the strength of it. Ezri could spend the rest of her life contemplating possibilities that others had created, or she could create her own, by choosing to follow her heart.

The joining of Ezri Tigan and Dax loved Julian Bashir, very much. If he survived, and he would, *he will,* she was going to make a place for him in her life, period; she could find her space to grow, but she couldn't find another Julian. If he died, she would lose her closest friend, and a lover who made her feel good about herself, who loved Ezri Dax.

That can't happen, it can't.

Shaking, Ezri held her blood-smeared hands together against her abdomen, watching as two nurses and a doctor fought for his life. After a moment, someone else gently asked her to wait outside, and Ezri managed to make her legs carry her away, telling herself that he would be fine, that everything would be fine now.

II

With Geordi and Data leading the maintenance teams and the captain in the station's wardroom, talking to Starfleet, Will Riker really had nothing to do on the bridge but stand around as CO of a communications noncom and an engineering tech. He was impatient to take his own leave, looking forward to winding down, still not recovered from the news about the *Aldebaran.* He stared at the blank main screen, waiting for the captain to return.

The *Enterprise* was officially inactive, the warp cores undergoing a definitive diagnostic, the subspace arrays still offline. The captain hadn't liked it any more than Will did, the nearly complete power down with the wormhole so nearby, but the *I.K.S. Tcha'voth,* Vor'cha-class, was still standing guard, and repairs had to be made.

Particularly if we're going to join up with this

task force to the Gamma Quadrant. Riker hadn't liked that much, either; an armed investigation into the Gamma Quadrant seemed like a monumentally foolish idea. No one knew how the Dominion was taking their defeat, and it seemed to him that moving aggressively into the Gamma Quadrant to confront them after three silent months wasn't going to make things less tense.

And there's the Jem'Hadar's story. Picard had told him about it upon his return to the *Enterprise,* and had gone to talk to Admiral Ross about the news. Deanna had just left to see who to talk to about offering assistance in an assessment. They were all keeping their fingers crossed that the Jem'Hadar was telling the truth.

The captain seemed to be in full agreement about the task force, after he heard Will's report on the update from Starfleet. Although he hadn't given a final opinion, wanting to hear the Federation's decision directly from Ross, Picard had clearly stated that he was leaning toward Kira's view of things, much the same as Will's. A few rogue ships on a suicide run had gotten lucky, turning a postwar skirmish into an interstellar incident. Such things needed to be handled carefully.

He was still thinking about it when Mr. Truke spoke up, his voice high with urgency, the fur on the back of his neck ruffling.

"Sir, I'm receiving multiple reports from crew on the station, that DS9 has just gone to red alert," he said, and Riker was up and moving, going to stand behind communications, watching the flatscreen for details. The crew members on the station would already be on their way back to the ship to sign in, standard procedure for an emergency while on leave.

Behind them, the door to the bridge opened and the captain walked in, finishing a call on his combadge. Although he wasn't speaking loudly, his voice resonated, his commanding tone at full force.

". . . than those we discussed, and inform her that we'll be standing by for anything else she needs," Picard said, striding toward his chair. "Thank you, Commander, Picard out."

The captain didn't sit down, turning to Riker instead. "That was Commander Vaughn. The Jem'Hadar soldier killed two guards and has escaped, the station is at red alert. Contact Data and Geordi, Number One, tell them we need our impulse engines back up immediately. I want us prepared if the need to provide evacuation transport arises. I'm going to ask Dr. Crusher to lend a hand at the station's infirmary, as it seems that the chief medical officer has been wounded. I want armed security teams standing by, to be called in if Lieutenant Ro requires them, she's chief of security. Make sure everyone understands that they're to accept direction from the station officers, rank notwithstanding; we want to assist, not get in the way."

*—Ro? Common name, someone else—*the thought barely rose from Will's subconscious before settling back.

Picard left him in com, going to his ready room. Riker hit his badge for Data, letting his organizational skills come into play as he reflexively broke down the orders, deciding how best to fulfill them through a series of mental directions—get updated DS9 schematics to the transporter rooms, process sign-ins and -outs back into the duty roster, yellow alert status to override shift changes and standbys but not to battle stations, get an exact time for the impulse drive to be fully functional . . .

His deeper thoughts were of Deanna. She wouldn't have gone to see the Jem'Hadar before working things through with the station's counselor, he was sure of it, and she hadn't been gone for that long. Not long enough to be anywhere near a Jem'Hadar on a killing spree, one who might recognize a Betazoid as a threat—

Riker let it go, throwing himself into the work. Relaying orders successfully was a skill, and he could best contribute to the resolution of a crisis by managing the system, by making things happen appropriately. And the faster he worked, the sooner he'd be able to call Deanna, and make sure she was all right.

Deanna Troi had only just reached the Promenade when the station went to red alert. Although she was usually fine with her defenses, the mass emotional response to the alarm signal and flashing panels was incredibly loud, solid and fast—there were something like 7500 people on board—and she felt herself tensing, the smash of anxiety digging at her with prickly fingers, looking for a way in.

She stepped to the Promenade's outer wall between a meeting hall and the station's infirmary, leaning against it, taking several deep breaths. She was fine, she just needed a moment to reestablish her filters. A recorded loop explained to the hurrying streams of people that it was an internal security alert, to act accordingly.

For all of the *Enterprise* crew that meant an immediate return to the ship, but Deanna closed her eyes and centered herself instead, running through a minute or two of shield visualization, picturing herself wearing armor made of light. She wasn't minimizing the importance of what was happening; she had to keep herself well, or she wouldn't be able to function. If the *Enterprise* had urgent need of her, they would call.

A few more deep breaths, and Deanna opened her eyes, ready to go. There was a turbolift almost directly across from where she stood, to the right of a Spican jeweler's. She started toward the lift just as the doors opened, and Beverly stepped out. She was carrying her med kit and was unhappy, her energy brightening only a little when she saw Deanna approaching.

"Beverly, what's happening?"

Dismayed but not distressed, Beverly acted perfectly calm. "A Jem'Hadar soldier is loose on the station. He's killed two people and injured the CMO, he's in surgery now. Dr. Bashir, you remember him?"

Arrogant, childish, entirely charming and off-the-scale bright. He'd worked with Geordi to help Data "diagnose" his first dreams . . . eight years ago? It was the last time she'd seen him, anyway. Deanna nodded.

"The captain thought I might be able to help," Beverly said, a flush of concern coming from her, its nature . . . the doctor was afraid that more casualties were coming, Deanna thought.

"Why don't I come with you," Deanna half-asked, following an instinct, sure she could be useful in some capacity. Beverly was glad for the offer, which was enough of a reason.

As they walked across to the infirmary, people

hurrying by on either side, Deanna called in to the bridge. Will picked it up, and sounded relieved to know where she was. He didn't object to her continued absence from the ship, although he quietly told her to be careful after relaying the order of deference to station staff. She returned the sentiment and followed Beverly into the infirmary.

There were three medical attendants and a doctor from the Bajoran Militia in the infirmary's front room, loading hypos and bandages into med kits. A lone patient was being seen to by a fourth nurse; it appeared minor, the patient sitting on the edge of an exam table. A young woman with a liberal amount of blood on her uniform stood stonily near a set of doors to the right, which presumably led to surgery. She had smears of blood on her face. Deanna couldn't make her rank, but she was dressed in Starfleet sciences . . .

. . . and she's obviously a friend of Dr. Bashir's.

As Beverly approached the group packing med kits, Deanna let her emotional barriers soften toward the bloody young woman. She was traumatized and afraid, but also seemed to be incredibly focused, much too focused for her emotional state, or her age, for that matter. There was something strangely familiar about her, too, though Deanna felt sure that she'd never seen her before. The young woman stared straight ahead, her profile to Deanna, her arms crossed, expressionless.

Deanna took a step closer and saw that she was Trill, which explained the woman's precision of spirit; the distinctive markings were partly obscured by the bloody smudges on her face . . . and Deanna realized with a start that it had to be Dax.

Deanna and Worf had parted ways amicably enough, and although they hadn't faithfully kept in touch, she'd always wished him well. She'd met Jadzia Dax once, the woman who would eventually become his wife, and had liked her very much; she'd been pleased by the news of their wedding, the expected pang of jealousy lasting only a short time. The marriage itself had ended tragically, when Jadzia had been killed. Deanna had seen Worf only a month after that during the mission to Betazed, and she had wanted to reach out to him, to offer him that friendship they still shared; but as with so many other things, the crisis of the moment had made it impossible. She'd found out later from Keiko O'Brien that Worf had recently returned from a battle he'd fought in Jadzia's name.

And Keiko also mentioned that there was a new Dax aboard . . . and that she was a counselor.

Deanna didn't want to invade Dax's privacy; she sensed that the young woman was . . .

. . . in hope, in desperation, bargaining and affirming. In love . . . Her lover was in surgery. This incarnation of Dax was with Julian Bashir, it seemed, and she was working hard to believe that he was going to survive; Dax wasn't looking for company, she was trying to concentrate.

Deanna had just decided that she might be most useful back aboard the *Enterprise* after all, when a familiar female voice boomed over the Promenade com system, ordering the immediate evacuation of Deep Space 9.

12

After an overlong meal break, Shar had returned to ops feeling a new heaviness in each step, imagining that people were already looking at him differently. He knew that it was unlikely in so short a time, but couldn't help it. It had happened at the Academy, and again on the *Tamberlaine,* as soon as it got around who his "mother" was.

You ignore the real issue, he scolded himself, entering ops without looking at anyone, going straight to the science station. He hadn't wanted anyone to know his relationship to Charivretha, but what he wanted wasn't all that important, not to his family. There were times he felt it never had been.

He wished he had more time now, that he could afford to continue avoiding thoughts of his future, but knew that he was being irrational. *Zhavey*'s call, the first since he'd come to the station, had forced him to face the immediacy of his situation. He didn't like it, but couldn't pretend any longer that it did not exist.

I can, however, avoid thinking about it while I'm on shift. It was inappropriate for him to bring personal troubles with him to his work; it was what the Academy taught, and Shar thought it was sound instruction. He was in ops to keep working with the internal and external sensor arrays, to fine-tune and test all of the readjustments that had been made in the past few days. People depended on him to do his job well; he would not founder because of his own problems.

As soon as he finished looking over the array results from the past few hours, Shar logged a requisition for a new console to be installed in his quarters. He didn't list a reason, and hoped he wouldn't be questioned about it. As Nog had pointed out over their drinks, Shar didn't talk about a lot of things . . . but he didn't lie, either.

Ops was quiet, most of the manual repair work finished, the stations occupied but the colonel's office empty. He considered visiting the *Enterprise* after his shift ended. It was, after all, the ship that Data, Soong's son, served on, and Shar had always wanted to meet the android. But the idea failed to excite him; his violent outburst after the call from *Zhavey* had been draining, but the shame that had followed had been much worse, stealing even the carefully restrained satisfaction he took in his work. For the first time since he'd come to the station, he hadn't wanted to go to his shift. He knew it would pass, but knew also that until he could tell his family what they wanted to hear, the situation would only get worse. . . .

Shar felt his chest constrict with unhappiness, and he did what he could to forget all of it, his family, home, what was expected of him. If he could not enjoy his work, there was no point to all of his struggling.

He was almost an hour into checking the external sampling arrangement, so focused that nothing else existed, when Kira called tactical, issuing an internal security alert—the Jem'Hadar soldier had escaped.

Ops was suddenly in motion, everyone contacting their department teams and securing orders, struggling with backup communications as each worked to account for his or her people and equipment.

Within seconds, Shar went into a state of calm efficacy as his body adjusted to the circumstances, his thoughts refocusing to the tasks at hand. Tracking the Jem'Hadar could best be done from his console. Ignoring the internal visual arrays, he worked with the station's sensors to focus on energy fields and spatial displacement, starting from the cargo bay where the soldier had been held and extending outward. Unfortunately, without knowing which way the Jem'Hadar had gone, he couldn't exclude most of the station, nor could he rely decisively on what he was getting; there was nothing keeping the soldier from doubling back to an area that had been scanned, it was the same problem they'd had running the internal sweeps after Kitana'klan had been discovered, and with the station's energy shortages, blanketing large areas was practically impossible.

"Kira to sciences."

"Ch'Thane here," Shar answered.

"Shar—we're going to attempt to pick up Kitana'klan's trail by manually testing for graviton residue. I want you to focus on us, and stand by to search for Kitana'klan's shroud signature as soon as we establish direction."

"Yes, sir," Shar said, finding the team at the cargo bay before she'd finished speaking. There were eight lifesigns, one human and seven Bajorans, and they set out almost immediately, heading for the cargo transfer aisle that ran to the outer Habitat Ring.

Kitana'klan had been held in one of several storage areas at the base of pylon one, and when the team passed the pylon's main turbo shaft, Shar removed it from the search zone. It made no sense for the Jem'Hadar to go up pylon one, as there were no ships docked there . . . although that was assuming he actually meant to escape.

"Shar, are you still with us?" The colonel again.

"Yes, sir."

"Take upper pylon one off the possibility list, and start—wait, just a minute . . ."

Shar waited, the reason for Kira's hesitation glowing on his schematic in soft red. The team had reached a maintenance tunnel in the crossover bridge, moving toward the hub of the station. When Colonel Kira spoke again, he could hear the gathering apprehension in her voice.

"Stay with us. Keep narrowing the perimeter."

Watching the path they were following, Shar understood her trepidation. He heard Ensign Ahzed, at the engineering station, tell Kira that Lieutenant Nog was standing by at one of the cargo transporters, only waiting for the word to send the team to Kitana'klan's location.

Which is becoming clearer with each step they

take. Shar made no assumptions, but the trail was unwavering in its course, and he was fairly sure even before the colonel told him where to concentrate his efforts.

The Jem'Hadar was almost certainly in the lower core, where the fusion reactors were, where the multiple plasma conduits were still being repaired; the station had been on the less secure secondary system since the attack, the engineering teams creating a single central conduit surrounded by forcefield. It wouldn't take too much effort to completely obliterate the station by explosive overload, assuming one was so inclined; an increase in plasma density in the deuterium slush flow could create a cataclysmic overload in a matter of minutes.

It only took a minute and half for Shar to find the Jem'Hadar, but he'd already had more than enough time to tamper with the reactors; it had been nearly six minutes since the red alert panels on Shar's console had started to flash, and he didn't know how long Kitana'klan had been free before his absence was noted.

In his current state of enhanced objectivity and heightened awareness, Shar wasn't capable of fear for himself. But for the rest of the station, he grew more worried by the moment.

They were in a scarcely used service corridor at lower mid-core when Kira found she could no longer avoid the obvious. She halted the team, realizing that if she was right, they needed to start a full-scale evacuation immediately.

"Search the lower core," Kira told Shar. "Concentrate on paths to and from the reactors, and around the fusion core."

Kira turned to face the others, calculating time and necessity, hoping that she was wrong but seriously doubting it. Kitana'klan was going to try and blow up the station; she could think of no other reason that he would have run to the lower core. He'd lied about everything, and she'd wanted so badly to believe him that she hadn't taken enough precaution. And they were all going to suffer for it.

Blame yourself later.

"Ro, head to ops," she said, working out plans as she spoke. "I want you to begin emergency evacuation procedures on the way. Call in everyone you need to get it done as quickly as possible. Have communications contact every ship in our immediate vicinity except for the *Tcha'voth* and tell them to get out of blast range, assume full-scale. Have Shar coordinate with the *Enterprise* and the *Tcha'voth* for whatever evacuation transport they can provide, we've got seventy-five hundred on board, and between the two of them, they can . . ."

Kira trailed off, staring at Ro, who gazed back at her with a kind of terror-struck awe, her usually impassive face expressing a depth of feeling that Kira had never seen before. Seventy-five hundred, give or take. Something like a thousand on the *Enterprise,* nearly two thousand on the *Tcha'voth*—

"Ten thousand," Ro breathed, and Kira felt a deep chill hearing it said aloud, one that went into her bones. She'd assumed the prophecy had meant ten thousand *Bajorans*—it said that ten thousand of the land's children would die, but between the two starships and the station, the number was too close. If only a half-dozen escape pods made it out, the number might even be exact.

But it's heresy, part of her objected, *and Kasidy is on the station, the rest of the prophecy can't come true if she dies.*

Maybe she won't die. Maybe she'll be saved. Maybe it'll just be the rest of us.

"Go," Kira said. It was the only answer. They had to stop Kitana'klan, whatever he was doing. DS9 was not going to be lost because of one soldier. Or one heretical prophecy.

Ro nodded, her anxious expression hardening to determination. "Yes, sir."

She turned and hurried away, already talking into her combadge.

Kira turned to Vaughn. "Commander, it might be a good idea if you—"

"All due respect, Colonel, but I may know more about the Jem'Hadar than anyone else here," he interrupted, his jaw firmly set. Kira wasn't going to argue.

"Colonel, I have him," Shar said, and the five guards immediately moved closer together, Vaughn and Kira both stepping in with them.

"It appears that he's at the fusion core, on grid twenty-two," Shar added.

Where the primary reactor banks are.

"Get us to twenty-one," Kira said, pulling her phaser, nodding at her team. "Set phasers on maximum."

Seconds later, the corridor sparkled away.

* * *

When Ahzed in ops told him that the soldier had escaped, Nog didn't feel vindicated. He felt nauseated and angry and afraid, telling the ensign that he would handle the security team's transport personally before hurrying from the *Defiant* to the closest docking-ring transporter system. He informed ops that he was standing by at one of the larger cargo transports, and someone sent him the team's signature signals, and then he could only wait and worry, alone. He felt cold and shaky, his stomach strangely empty-feeling, the rims of his ears burning with anxiety.

I was right, nobody listened but I was right all along, he told himself, staring blankly at the CPG controls, his hands trembling just a little. Still, no sense of self-righteous indignation, no glimmer of smarmy satisfaction beneath his fear. As he waited for the word, he thought that he would happily forswear all material wealth for the rest of his life to have been wrong. The monster was loose, and when the destination coordinates for the team flashed across his console's screen, Nog actually groaned out loud.

The core! And only one level above the main reactor banks. With the six reactor conduits still offline, the energy flow to the station was coming from a single, central channel. Easier to sabotage and with more explosive results.

"Energize," Ahzed said, and Nog did it, promising himself that he would never again back down when he knew he was right, wishing that he'd learned that particular lesson a long time ago.

13

As soon as they transported, Kira raised one hand, circled in the air with her finger, then pointed down. The grid they were on was exactly that, although the holes were small and spaced far apart; they would have to move to the edge and look over the railing to see the level below.

They had materialized on grid 21, one of the many mesh walkways that surrounded the secondary plasma channel in a series of reinforced metal arcs. The brilliant, glowing mass of moving energy was gigantic, an elongated column suspended through the middle of the lower core shaft and held in place by forcefields. The combined energy from the reaction chambers was still only two-thirds of what the station was used to, it had been since the attack, but the destructive potential was no less. If the core were to overload, the station and anything within a hundred kilometers of it would be blown to atoms.

The twenty-first level of open walkways and platforms was closer to the base of the channel than to the top; the clear conduit extended high over their heads, at least eighty meters of it, and another twenty below. The air was cold, the vast chamber strangely lit by the brilliant spire of white-flame-colored, pulsating power. A deep, throbbing hum resounded throughout the shaft, providing a blanket of white noise that seemed to vibrate the very air.

Together, Kira and Vaughn leading the way, the team sidled toward the railing, only five or six meters from the outside of the glowing tower. At various intervals up and down the core shaft, red alert panels flashed silently, their blinking crimson light barely noticeable in the vivid blaze of the massive conduit.

Kira darted a glance over the side, looking down and to the left, tightly gripping her phaser—

—and there he was. Unshrouded, kneeling in front of the first bank of reactor panels, Kitana'klan had his arms thrust into an open vent near the bottom of the system capacitance section. A phaser lay on the platform next to him . . . and only a few meters away, the broken body of an engineer, obviously dead. A male Bajoran she didn't recognize, probably one of the techs who'd come in on the shuttle.

Kira felt a sudden surge of hate for the Jem'Hadar, sick with the fact that she had been even partially fooled by such a creature; he'd surely been on one of the attack ships, already responsible for mass murder. He had killed two young officers and perhaps Julian in his escape, and now a civilian, a man who had voluntarily come to the station to lend his skills, to help rebuild what Kitana'klan had already tried to destroy once.

And there he is, efficiently working away to finish us off, oblivious to everything else. Kira had tried hard in her life to learn forgiveness for, or at least understanding of, her enemies, but Kitana'klan didn't deserve his life. She wanted him dead, and the sooner the better.

She looked at Vaughn, who held up his own phaser, nodding, his eyes narrowing as he took another look at the unknowing saboteur. Safest to kill him outright, then undo whatever he was doing to the reactors.

Kira jabbed a finger at Sergeant Wasa, beckoning for him to take aim; Wasa Graim was probably the most accurate shot on the station, and had trained half of the security force. A mostly solemn man in his early fifties, Wasa edged to the railing, carefully raised his phaser—

—and before he could fire, Kitana'klan was moving, scooping up his own weapon as he threw himself sideways into a shoulder roll, so fast that he almost seemed a blur as he disappeared under their grid. Wasa took a shot before the Jem'Hadar was entirely out of sight, missing the soldier's heels by scant centimeters. The phaser blast skidded harmlessly across the metal grating.

Damn! She didn't know how he'd known, but it didn't matter now, they had to—

It happened so quickly.

Kitana'klan was suddenly in sight again, dancing out from beneath the grid just long enough to fire, disappearing before any one of them could get off a shot—or get out of the way.

Wasa went down, dead before he hit the floor, a

blackened circle appearing almost dead center on his chest. And with a single running step back across the platform, Kitana'klan ducked among the banks of machinery again. If he stayed low, they wouldn't be able to spot him from their position.

"Back, get back," Kira whispered harshly, thinking fast, remembering something that Vaughn had said when they'd first starting talking, about the superiority of a Jem'Hadar's reflexes. He was fast, and deadly with a phaser, and now Graim was no more; they couldn't hope to outshoot him.

A trap, something he won't suspect . . . She looked down at Graim and offered a silent prayer, fighting not to think of his two teenaged daughters.

Kira huddled with Vaughn and the four security guards against the shaft wall, silently commending the team for the determination she saw in their grim faces. Vaughn spoke first, his voice low and hurried as he addressed Kira.

"He's going to stay there, to protect his work for as long as he can or as long as he feels is necessary. If you can distract him, draw his fire up here, I might be about to circle down and get behind him."

"My thoughts exactly," Kira said. "But I'm going." The walkway they stood on led to platforms on either side, those connecting to more extensive passages across the core—and several runged ladders, in addition to the four half-caged lifts that ran the length of the shaft.

"We should both go," Vaughn said. "Or three of us, but not together. He'll expect one or all of us to go straight at him, not two or three coming from different directions."

So if he kills one, he'll think he's safe. She didn't want anyone else to die, but if it meant saving the station, she was ready.

Kira nodded, glancing at the others, deciding that she and Vaughn would try it alone; more people meant more noise.

"Make it look good, revolving shots, not a constant barrage," she said. "Don't hit any equipment. Keep firing until we get to the banks."

They were all nodding, but she could see the question in their eyes, as plain as stars at night.

"If we don't make it, call for additional security," she said, answering what she knew no one would ask. "We have to stop him, we have to disable whatever he did to the main controls."

Although if Vaughn and I don't get him, it may be too late. She wasn't sure what Kitana'klan had done, but he must have known they'd find him within minutes of his escape. Whatever his exact plans, he was obviously confident that he wouldn't be stopped before he saw them to fruition.

With a silent prayer that the evacuation was going well, Kira and Vaughn separated from the team, heading away from Kitana'klan's position toward the other side of the cavernous shaft. Behind them, the team began to fire.

When they reached the first of the wall ladders across from the team, hoping that the tower of transforming matter would block them from the Jem'Hadar's sight, Vaughn signaled that he would take it, that she should pick another route down. Whoever reached the lower platform first was more likely to be hit. He didn't have a suicide wish, but one of them had to go first, and Kira commanded the station, her survival was more important than his.

Kira must have realized it, too. She didn't look happy but she didn't hesitate, either; she nodded, pointing at herself and then at another ladder several meters away, near one of the lifts. If she was afraid, he hadn't seen it. Kira Nerys was cooler under pressure than some Starfleet admirals he'd known.

Still holding his phaser, Vaughn stepped down onto the rungs, quickly and quietly one-arming it to the bottom. When he reached the lower grid he turned, deciding the best approach to the reactor bank area. Neither way looked promising, the walkways and platforms all open, the only real cover provided by the power conduit; heading to the right seemed fractionally safer, there looked to be a secondary reactor station, a few solid control banks that could act as a temporary screen.

Vaughn looked up, and saw Kira waiting to see which way he would go, her face a pale, half-shadowed oval by the light of the central conduit. He pointed to himself and then to the left; she nodded, then disappeared from view. Above them, more phaser fire erupted. Kitana'klan wasn't firing back, and Vaughn seriously doubted it was because he'd been injured or killed.

Let's do this. His heart was pounding, his body itching with adrenaline. No matter how many times he'd walked into deadly situations, it was never something that one could get used to. He'd known other humans who'd insisted they felt no fear, but as far as he was concerned, they were either lying or fools.

Crouching, Vaughn sidestepped his way to his left, alert to even a hint of sound or motion. The constant thrum of the reactors would cover any small sounds, but even well-trained Jem'Hadar weren't known for their subtlety. If Kitana'klan took him out, he'd make enough noise so that Kira would at least have an idea of his location. And even a shrouded Jem'Hadar couldn't hide from a phaser sweep.

Vaughn edged around the conduit, the main reactor banks sliding into view. He could see the dead man and the console that had been tampered with, but no Jem'Hadar. Another volley of brilliant phaser fire stabbed down from above, the shots still too wide; the security team hadn't happened across their target yet.

Go, now!

While they were firing, Vaughn ran, taking advantage of the fact that Kitana'klan wasn't likely to stick his head up to take a look around. There was a narrow storage locker only a few meters from the reactor bank platform, situated at a widened section of the walkway. Vaughn reached it and squatted in its shadow, darting another look at how the reactor banks were situated.

Three long rows, say seven meters each and four individual units, nothing taller than two meters . . . Kitana'klan would either be somewhere he could fire on anyone approaching his handiwork, or close enough to the front row to attack physically. Either way, going straight in was definitely a risk, and one they had no choice but to take. Time was a factor.

So take a risk. He could run past the ends of all three rows, firing down each. If he stayed low, he might get lucky . . .

. . . but the odds are a lot better that he'll get me, first. Vaughn would have to hesitate before each shot, just long enough to be sure that Kira wasn't in the line of fire—but that fraction of a second would be all that Kitana'klan needed.

And my death would be all that Kira needs to find him. He wasn't sure where Kira was, but she was certainly close by now. If his sacrifice meant saving thousands of lives, the choice was simple.

When all of the security team members started firing again, he launched himself from behind the cabinet, crouch-running for the rows of equipment, phaser ready.

Vaughn had just reached the first machines when he heard Kira cry out in surprise and pain, the sound cut off a second later when he heard a deep and loud, echoing *crunch,* and something landed heavily on the platform.

Kira was behind a low console not far from the main banks, and was just readying herself to make a run across the open platform when she saw Vaughn. The commander was making a break for the equipment banks, crouching low, a look of fierce determination on his face.

If they both ran at Kitana'klan, wherever he was among the reactor instrumentation, he could only kill one of them at a time.

Go! Kira launched out from behind her shelter—

—and felt brutal, shocking pain as invisible claws

punctured her waist on either side, the crushing force of the grip stealing her breath.

Kira swung both of her arms forward, hitting only air, *behind me—*

—and before she could fire into the space behind her, before she even got her arm up, she heard at least one of her ribs snapping as the shrouded creature squeezed, a terrible, internal bone-sound. She started to cry out and then she was in motion, flying, the console rushing up to meet her face as Kitana'klan threw her into the secondary bank. She felt the right side of her head hitting solid plasticine, she felt something in her upper right arm give way in a wave of dark pain—

Vaughn spun around, the sound coming from near the secondary station where he'd sent Kira so that she might have a better chance—and that was also effectively blocked from the security team's line of fire. They'd stopped firing anyway, as soon as Vaughn had reached the main banks.

He leaned against the end of the front row and shot a look around the corner, silently cursing when he saw Kira's boots sticking out from behind the low console. Acting on reflex, he triggered his phaser and swept it across the open platform a meter and a half off the floor, the bright beam searing the shaft wall before crackling brilliantly across the conduit's forcefield.

Nothing. Kitana'klan would have unshrouded if he'd been hit. *Behind the console? Circling around the core?* Vaughn couldn't randomly fire, couldn't risk damaging the vital controls of the fusion reactors, and the soldier could be anywhere.

He needed to get to the machine that Kitana'klan

had worked on, his instincts screaming that time was running out. He'd have to call the security team down, even knowing that some or all of them would be killed trying to get to the sabotaged controls. Beyond that—

—beyond that, I call Picard and Ro and tell them to get the hell away from here.

Vaughn reached for his combadge—and felt a hot breath on the back of his neck, and knew he was as good as dead.

With at least twenty platforms to descend, he'd been too late to stop Kitana'klan from hurting the Bajoran Kira Nerys. Once again, he had not anticipated correctly. His failures had already caused enough death; the obvious recourse was to cease failing. Taran'atar quickly moved to be near the silver-haired human, understanding that the whelp would try to kill him next. The human's uniform indicated he was a Starfleet commander with a specialty in command or strategic operations, and therfore a priority target.

Only Jem'Hadar could sense the *di'teh,* the aura of the shrouded, and even then only if they were physically very close. But he remained undetected as he held his position next to the commander; Kitana'klan was too distracted, too intent on his next victim to sense Taran'atar's presence. It was as close as they'd been since their arrival, the best opportunity he'd had with the consistently wary soldier; even as the Starfleet human tensed, Taran'atar was in motion.

He unshrouded as he grabbed Kitana'klan by the throat, holding on tight and diving for the floor. The unsuspecting young soldier was thrown off balance. He hit the platform awkwardly, half on his back, becoming visible as he struggled to get free of Taran'atar's grasp, his concentration faltering.

Kitana'klan was strong and fast but too young, unaware that his lethal rage wasn't enough. Still holding him by the throat, Taran'atar swung himself over the youth's thrashing body, straddling his chest.

Kitana'klan snatched at Taran'atar's throat and face, kicking at his back, his pale eyes shining with murder. The blows were powerful but poorly executed, barely effective. Taran'atar looked down into the young soldier's twisted, ignorant face, and saw himself a long, long time ago.

"Accept death," Taran'atar said, but Kitana'klan still fought. A good soldier. Taran'atar moved his hands to the sides of Kitana'klan's pebbled skull, took a firm grip, and twisted, hard. There was an audible *crack*, a sound of tearing muscle, and Kitana'klan ceased to be.

The battle had lasted only seconds. Taran'atar smoothly rose to his feet, nodding at the silver-haired commander, whose eyes never wavered from his.

"I take it you're on our side," the human said.

"I am," Taran'atar confirmed, matching the commander's scrutiny. Silver hair usually represented older age in humans, he thought. Perhaps he was wise.

"Good to know," the commander said. "We can talk about it later."

The man shouted up at the four others not to fire as he hurriedly dropped to his knees in front of one of the machines, opening a wide panel. Taran'atar crouched next to him, ready to offer his assistance.

He thought they might be too late to stop whatever destructive plan Kitana'klan had set in motion; the light of the power channel had started to change, getting brighter, and there was a growing sound, a sound like machinery that was dying, but perhaps the commander could stop it in time.

Taran'atar hoped that it would be so. He could not atone for his mistakes if they all died.

The machine was Federation and it adjusted plasma density. Looking at the numbers on the small internal screen, Vaughn saw what Kitana'klan had done almost immediately. Behind them, the light was growing stronger, and Vaughn thought that the chamber's powerful hum was incrementally higher than before.

Damn damn damn!

The Jem'Hadar had instructed the system to increase density by twenty percent and then shorted the boards, including the alarm sensors. The structural integrity of the fusion reactors had been compromised, and the data indicated that the station's power grid had ceased to accept the unbalanced flow of energy. A buildup was already under way, but if Vaughn could get to the venting system, there might still be time to release the mounting pressure.

The Jem'Hadar who was not his enemy squatted at his side, and when Vaughn stood, so did he. Vaughn shouted up at the security team as he ran to the second bank of machines, the Jem'Hadar still with him.

"Evacuate!" Vaughn yelled, recognizing that they probably only had minutes, wondering why there weren't a hundred other alarms going off. "Get out of here, now, and tell everyone at least two hundred klicks away from the station!"

He didn't bother to see if they'd gone, hunting for the exhaust cone controls. He wasn't familiar with DS9's setup, but the equipment was all recognizable, and the hum *was* getting louder; it might already be too late to vent before the core went supercritical.

"I will aid you," the Jem'Hadar said, just as Vaughn spotted the controls for the cone.

"See if Kira's alive," Vaughn snapped, scanning the console's panels, feeling sweat run down his chest. *There,* emergency functions! Vaughn hit the key and a grid of options scrolled across the monitor. He saw the overload strip and jabbed at the touch square, praying for success—

—and the screen went blank.

No.

Vaughn saw the board access panel and yanked it open, already knowing what he would see. From the convoluted tangle of broken cables, he was surprised that the monitor had worked at all. Alarms weren't going off because it seemed that the Jem'Hadar had smashed the reactor sensor arrays all to hell, or at least the ones that would have triggered an overload alert.

Vaughn couldn't know how much time they had, he didn't know the core capacity or how well the station's systems worked, but he guessed five or six minutes at the outside. They still had time to get to a ship, to get away, but he could hardly see the point; even if the evacuation had been running like clockwork, he doubted very much that more than a few thousand people had managed to get out. Leaving the doomed station, leaving thousands more to die as they commandeered a private ship, seemed cowardly and arrogant.

Vaughn slammed his fist against the useless console, feeling just as useless.

There was no way for anyone to stop it. DS9 was going to explode.

Someone was touching her face.

Kira swam up from the dark sea, feeling terrible, feeling as though she was going to vomit from the pain in her head. The left side of her body felt strange, far away, and when she tried to move, her right arm went white-hot with agony.

She opened her eyes and saw Kitana'klan bending over her, the back of one cold, scaled hand pressed against her forehead. She tried to move away, but her body wasn't listening, her motor skills malfunctioning.

Kitana'klan spoke, but his voice was garbled, only a few clear words reaching her.

". . . station . . . not . . . killed the . . . fusion . . ."

The station. She remembered parts of what had happened, but her head hurt so much, and she didn't understand what Kitana'klan was saying, let alone why he was talking to her at all, and there was a high-pitched whine in her ears—

—hum, rising hum, Kitana'klan was at the reactor banks—

—overload?

The thought was more important than her pain. She struggled to sit up, ignoring the torment of her upper right arm, and there was Commander Vaughn, next to her, next to Kitana'klan.

"Help me up," she said, but her voice didn't

work, her own words as foreign as the Jem'Hadar's. She tried again, and was now aware that the light around her was getting brighter, that things might be very bad.

"Help . . . up," she managed. Her voice was slurred, and she understood that she'd taken a blow to the head, but didn't care. She didn't care that her assailant, along with Vaughn, was gently easing her into an upright position, and she didn't care about the pain. The station, she had to know what was happening.

". . . core overload, the . . . won't vent," Vaughn babbled.

Kira concentrated as hard as she could, understanding that things *were* bad, they were critical. There had to be something . . .

. . . get away from it. Get it away.

If there wasn't any way to stop it from happening, there was only one option left.

"Get me up," she slurred. "Lift. Eject it from the top, my voice. Jettison. Up, we go up."

She must have made sense, Vaughn was talking to the soldier excitedly, and although she didn't want Kitana'klan to touch her, she couldn't stop him from picking her up, cradling her like a child. But she didn't care about that, either.

The station. The station.

Colonel Kira Nerys spoke, her words vague but her voice strong with urgency. Taran'atar understood each word, but didn't know what they meant. The commander apparently did.

"We have to get to the top of the shaft, now," he

said, no less urgently than the colonel. "Can you pick her up?"

Taran'atar did so. The colonel was light in his arms, and obviously suffering from a head injury. He could see the swollen flesh just above her right ear, and her eyes were blurred with pain; he thought her arm was broken, too. It was bad, that he'd let this happen.

"Hurry, to that lift," the commander said, and Taran'atar held Kira Nerys tighter, running to the caged platform. The rising sound of imminent overload and the now sickly-white light that bathed the shaft lent him speed; death was close for them all.

The colonel gritted her teeth against the jostling motion, but did not cry out or lose consciousness. A good soldier, for a Bajoran.

Odo had not exaggerated her strength.

Vaughn slammed the lift controls as soon as they were inside—and the open platform, surrounded by a waist-high railing, began to move up, slowly, very slowly. It would take almost a full minute to reach mid-core. He could call for transport, but wanted anyone at the transporter controls to be concentrating on the evacuation. And by the time their moving signals were locked on to, considering the signal interference that was surely being caused by the power build, they'd have already reached the top.

The growing whine of the imminent overload was joined now by a recorded loop, a woman's voice explaining that there was an emergency situation. Her calm voice resounded through the core chamber.

"Warning. Plasma temperature is unstable. Engage liquid sodium loop at emergency venting. Capacity overload will occur in five minutes. Warning. Plasma temperature . . ."

Vaughn tuned it out, willing the lift to hurry.

The Jem'Hadar stood stiffly as if at attention, his impassive gaze fixed on Vaughn, Kira barely conscious in his arms. Vaughn hadn't had time to wonder about the soldier's fortuitous appearance, but as the lift slowly ascended, he remembered Kira's account of the Jem'Hadar strike against the station.

Three ships firing, and one that tried to stop them. All Vaughn knew for sure was that he'd killed Kitana'klan, and that made him an ally.

They were almost to the top, only a few more levels and the lift would reach the base of the station's middle section.

Vaughn reached out and touched Kira's pale face, hoping to any god or prophet who might be watching that she'd be able to function long enough to authorize the lower core break. Her eyes were shut and her forehead was creased, but whether it was in pain or concentration Vaughn couldn't be sure. Her injuries were severe; it was astounding that she'd managed to speak at all. Her solution hadn't occurred to him, DS9 hadn't been built by Starfleet, but her stilted command had been clear enough—although he feared her voice wouldn't be, that the computer might not recognize her faltering commands.

". . . loop at emergency venting. Capacity overload will occur in four minutes."

Even if Kira could pull it off, how long would it take for the fusion core to reach a safe distance?

The lift passed the very top of the straining fuel tower, passed open space, rising through a mostly solid landing. They came to a stop in a circular room lined with blinking lights and flashing consoles. For the first time since coming aboard, Vaughn was struck by the true immensity of the station.

With an obvious effort, Kira forced her eyes open as soon as the lift stopped moving, as Vaughn slammed the low gate open and they stepped out. Ominous light filtered up from the lower core in shafts, the flashing red glow of the emergency panels combining to make unclean shadows.

"Master con," she said, blinking hard. They almost couldn't hear her over the now piercing whine of the overload.

Vaughn looked wildly around the room, spotting the main computer bank at eleven o'clock.

"Over there!"

Taran'atar ran at his side; Kira gritted her teeth against pain as they stopped in front of the master console.

"Down," she said, and Vaughn helped Taran'atar lower her feet to the floor, both of them supporting her.

". . . overload will occur in three minutes," the computer noted.

Kira forced her eyes open and saw the controls. The station. The lower core. There was a horrible, wavering sound, high-pitched, like machinery that was about to burst apart from overheating.

My station. My people.

"Hit three-one-four-seven-zero," she whispered,

and a hand reached out to the controls, hurriedly punching the code in. She wanted to crumble, to go to sleep, but Kitana'klan held her up and she knew that it was the end. One chance, and then it was over.

Concentrate! The voice of every teacher she'd ever had, every commander, the voice of authority shouting in her aching head. *Do it, get this done, don't fail!*

"Computer, this is Colonel Kira Nerys, initiate . . . initiate lower core emergency separation," she said. It took all of her energy to speak. "Authorization Kira Alpha . . . One Alpha."

"Identity confirmed. Request additional authorization."

Kira closed her eyes. "Override, Kira Zero-Nine. Disengage and initiate emergency launch . . . on my mark. *Mark.*"

Did it, got it done . . . Kira's head rolled to her chest, too heavy to hold up, but she kept herself awake; she had to know. And within seconds, she did.

There was a tremendous buckling beneath them, the strange, fierce light from below swirling into shadow with a sound of immense destruction, of meter-thick support beams snapping like twigs, of applied force and ruin. Kira tried to open her eyes and it was dark, she didn't know if the lights had gone out or if she'd managed to open them at all—but that terrible screeching sound had stopped, and she knew that it really was over.

"Did it," she mumbled, so tired that she thought she might sleep forever. And a minute later, when the jettisoned core exploded some 120 kilometers away in a blinding and spectacular blossom of devastation, when what was left of the station shuddered and rocked in the dark, pushed from its position by more than a dozen klicks, Kira Nerys slept on. There were no dreams.

14

In all, the injuries from the shock wave had been minor. Crusher had treated three broken arms, a couple of dislocations, and what seemed like a hundred minor lacs and contusions. They'd also had at least a dozen stress patients, all civilian, but nothing a mild sedative couldn't relieve; once Dr. Bashir was out of the woods, Ezri Dax had also lent a few calming words to the frightened men and women who'd dropped by. The other doctors and infirmary staff had been a pleasure to work with . . . most especially Simon Tarses, who, to her delighted surprise, was now a full MD. And as the small hours of the morning crept up on them, all the beds were clear except for three.

Not bad for a night's work. Crusher was tired but content, and although she didn't have to stay, she found herself lingering, enjoying the calm. Word was that everyone was back on the station now, which likely meant no more patients for a while; she imagined that DS9 was sleeping, thousands of people curled up in the safety of their beds. . . .

Crusher yawned, leaning against a wall near the supply cabinets. She knew better. With the station running entirely on backup, there were undoubtedly plenty of people working to stabilize systems and revise repair plans. It was just that curling up in bed sounded so heavenly at the moment—

"Dr. Crusher?"

It was Bashir, again. It was true that doctors made the worst patients. Bashir was pleasant enough about it, but he'd asked twice in the last hour if he could get up.

Crusher moved to the foot of his bed, catching a knowing glance from Dax in the soft glow of the emergency lights. She'd been at his side since he'd come out of surgery, not even leaving to change out of her bloody clothes; at some point she'd grabbed a scrub shirt and donned it where she sat.

"Yes, Doctor," Crusher said, smiling a little.

"My BP and hematocrit are both within normal range, and I'm certain the tissue stitch has set by now," he said, all seriousness. "*I* would release me."

"And if you were on duty, you could do that," she answered. "Another half hour, Julian. Postsurgical standards apply to everyone."

The young doctor sighed dramatically, but didn't argue, turning to gaze up at Dax instead; she smiled, stroking his hair. He'd been incredibly lucky, managing to get a seal patch over his right subclavian artery while he'd been in the process of bleeding to death. He said he couldn't remember it, that he was certain he'd passed out, but there was no other explanation.

Crusher left the young lovers to themselves, wandering over to check on the infirmary's other two patients, both asleep. Another human male, John Tiklak, who'd pitched over a railing when the station had been buffeted by the initial blast, one of his four broken ribs puncturing his left lung, also a fractured navicular of the left wrist; and Kira Nerys, concussion, open humeral fracture, two broken ribs. The concussion had bruised Kira's right temporal lobe, the injury severe enough that she was fortunate not to have suffered any permanent damage. Commander Vaughn had brought her in, explaining that like Bashir, the colonel had been injured by the Jem'Hadar soldier. Crusher hadn't gotten the full story; Vaughn had been in a rush over something and had stayed only long enough to hear that Kira would survive.

Speaking of.

The colonel was waking up, shifting beneath the coverlet, the reads over her bed showing a rise in consciousness. Beverly went to her side, wondering if Colonel Kira would remember that she'd saved the station. From the location of her concussion, Beverly thought it remarkable that the woman had managed to authorize the core ejection; speech, language comprehension, and gross motor skills would have all been affected.

Kira opened her eyes, frowning, and sat up.

"Easy, Colonel," Crusher said, smiling at her, speaking calmly. "I'm Beverly Crusher, the CMO from the *Enterprise;* I believe we met once, several years ago."

Kira nodded, still frowning. "I remember. How's the station? Was anyone hurt?"

Obviously, she was cognizant. "Colonel, everything is fine. You were badly injured by the Jem'Hadar, a concussion and several fractures, but you've been treated, and—"

"Picard to Dr. Crusher."

Still smiling at the young colonel, Beverly tapped her com. "Yes, Captain."

"Is Colonel Kira awake? The task force will be arriving in just a few minutes, and Commander Vaughn has called for a briefing as soon as the colonel is able to attend."

Kira was nodding. Crusher would have recommended a full night's sleep, but she was well enough—and Crusher suspected that the colonel wasn't the type to rest when there was station business to be handled. Kira had that in common with Jean-Luc—the belief that unless you were dying, there was no good excuse to delegate your own responsibilities. "Yes, Captain, she just woke up," Crusher said.

"Good. Please inform her that we're meeting in the station's wardroom. Admiral Ross and representatives from the Klingon and Romulan Empires will be meeting us."

Kira leaned and spoke in the direction of Crusher's combadge. "Captain, this is Kira. I'll need a few minutes to confer with my staff before I can be there."

"Of course," Picard said, and Crusher could hear the smile in his voice. "I look forward to it, Colonel. Picard out."

"Am I good to go?" Kira asked, leaning back and swinging her legs over the side of the bed. Dax and

Bashir both watched from across the room, holding hands and smiling.

"Absolutely. If you feel nausea or any vertigo, I want you back here, though, right away."

"Thank you, Doctor. And thank you for helping out here."

Crusher nodded, thinking of how different Kira looked awake. Asleep, her face had been as peaceful and lovely as a child's. As soon as she'd opened her eyes, her prettiness had become beauty; a level of intensity had been added, a kind of casual confidence and determination that matured her, defining her as a leader.

Kira stood and stretched, then walked over to Dax and Bashir, stopping to talk for a moment. Crusher could see the easy friendship between the three of them, the bond of working and living together in a closed community, and thought of her own friends, and how much she cherished them; Will and Deanna, Jean-Luc, Data and Geordi, her own staff of doctors and nurses and med techs. . . .

She yawned again, smiling at herself. She tended to get sentimental when she was tired. After checking one last time on John Tiklak and seeing that he was already in the capable, caring hands of Dr. Tarses, she put a friendly hand on Simon's shoulder. He looked into her warmly smiling face and smiled back, their shared relief needing nothing more. Then Crusher packed her med kit and went home.

Kira stopped at her quarters for a change of clothes, talking to Shar as she undressed, to Nog as she donned a fresh uniform, and to Bowers as she quickly brushed her rumpled hair. Shar relayed Ro's report, which included the news that the *Tcha'voth* had retrieved the escape pods that had launched; that the partial evacuation and subsequent return to the station had gone smoothly; and that everyone was accounted for. Except for a Bajoran citizen who'd been working in the lower core, a man named Alle Tol. That Kitana'klan had killed only four people during his escape was a small miracle, but Kira doubted that would prove a comfort to Tol's family. She would pray for them.

The upshot of all of the reports was that the station was safe. There had been no new structural damage from the lower core detonation, and although DS9 could operate temporarily with all the emergency generators running at full . . . there was still grim reality to face. Unless they could replace the reactor core in the short term, the station would no longer be viable.

One thing at a time.

Kira asked Shar to organize a senior staff meeting for 0900, deciding that they could all use a little extra time in the morning, to recover from the near catastrophe and get some much-needed rest. With Kitana'klan's story having proved to be a lie, she knew they were in for a few tense days or even weeks; the task force would press on with their investigation. If anything, they'd be even more insistent after hearing what Kitana'klan had attempted . . .

. . . except I really thought he was there at the end, with Vaughn. I remember him carrying me. An hallucination, it had to be; she felt fine now, just a little tired, but she'd been in a bad way after the head in-

jury. Julian and Ezri had told her that Kitana'klan was dead, that they'd heard it from Commander Vaughn, who had also spread the word that she had been entirely responsible for saving the station. As soon as she'd signed off from Shar, Kira was ready to head for her meeting. But as she turned, she caught sight for the first time of the spectacle outside her window.

The Allied task force, a combined armada of Federation, Klingon, and Romulan ships, far more than she'd expected. She'd prayed she would never again see such a thing in her lifetime . . . because a force like that had only one use, and she knew from personal experience what it was capable of.

Kira hurried out to Vaughn's meeting.

On her way, several people stopped her to ask how she was feeling, or to lend a thought about the generous nature of the Prophets. She'd been unconscious for only a couple of hours, but word had spread—and as much as she welcomed the feelings of community and faith, almost all of the Bajorans she talked to had questions about the book of prophecy. Questions she wasn't prepared to answer.

And now that the immediate crisis of Kitana'klan is over . . .

There was still Yevir, and the book, and the station's strange parallel to the Avatar prophecy . . . what if it *was* meant to come true, in some other way? And while Yevir's patronizing anger hadn't had much of an effect, Kira still had to come to terms with Kasidy's reaction, which had been far worse than she'd expected; she'd foolishly hoped that Kas would be pleased by the upload, happy to see Bajor growing and changing.

There's the Orb of Memory, though. Surely it's a sign, that exposing Bajor to Ohalu's book was the right thing to do.

Maybe it was, Kira thought, stepping into the turbolift. But doing the right thing didn't mean there were only positive consequences . . . and right or not, Kasidy's friendship was important to Kira; she should have talked to her before making any decision.

The turbolift reached the upper core and Kira quickly walked to the wardroom, hoping that Vaughn hadn't held the meeting up for her arrival; stopping to talk to people had slowed her down considerably. She wasn't sure, but thought that Vaughn had probably called the briefing to share his opinions on the task force; she hoped so, anyway. He clearly knew a lot about the Jem'Hadar, and if Picard was any indication, Vaughn was someone whose opinions counted among Starfleet brass.

As she rounded into the conference room's corridor, she saw that she *was* late. Four security guards stood outside the room, a Klingon, a Romulan, and two Starfleet. None of them looked happy to be sharing space with one another.

Nodding to the guards, Kira stepped inside the conference room—and froze, astonished by the scene.

Seated around the long meeting table were two Klingon captains, a Romulan commander, Admiral Ross, Captain Picard, and Commander Vaughn. All of them were looking at a uniformed Jem'Hadar soldier who stood near the head of the table, unrestrained, and no one had their weapons out.

"It's good to see you on your feet, Colonel," Vaughn began, rising from his chair, "but you may want to sit down. I'd like you to meet Taran'atar."

Although they'd asked him several questions, which he'd answered honestly, Taran'atar did not give a full account; Kira Nerys was the one with whom he'd been instructed to meet, and so he waited. When she finally arrived, Taran'atar felt an odd satisfaction that she had survived, of a duty fulfilled. She appeared to be well, and surprised to see him—although no more so than the others in the room had been. The Klingons had drawn weapons before the silver-haired human, Commander Vaughn, had explained his presence to them. Taran'atar thought it fortunate that the commander had intervened. Killing them would have run contrary to his task.

After Admiral Ross quickly made introductions, Vaughn again explained that it had been Taran'atar who had dispatched Kitana'klan, and helped both Kira and Vaughn in their last desperate moments with the lower core. Taran'atar stood and waited for him to finish, noting that Kira watched him almost the entire time.

Vaughn brought his narrative to a close, telling the colonel about Taran'atar's shrouded trip to the wardroom—in order to pass through the station without creating a panic—and Vaughn's decision to call the Allied leaders together, to hear what Taran'atar had to say. Taran'atar found himself wondering about the commander. It was curious; if his information on Alpha Quadrant command structures was accurate, Vaughn was the lowest-ranking officer in the room. Yet the other military leaders, especially the Starfleet officers, gave deference to him. Vaughn clearly did not command them, but they seemed to regard him as an equal, as if his rank were nothing more than a shroud.

". . . which brings us to the story of how he came to be here in the first place," Vaughn said. "Which I haven't heard, either. Taran'atar, will you speak to us now?"

"Yes," Taran'atar said, although he'd already decided that preparing for combat was much easier than addressing these aliens.

Victory is life. Conquer this unease, it is your enemy.

"The account Kitana'klan gave of how he came to be among you was partly true," he began, addressing Kira directly. "There was an envoy sent to your station as an envoy of peace, who was attacked by rogue Jem'Hadar who sought to thwart his mission. I am that envoy, chosen by the Founder Odo to live among you so that the Jem'Hadar might come to understand peaceful coexistence.

"After your war with the Dominion, Odo instructed the Vorta to begin a search among the Jem'Hadar for deviants. He believed, based upon knowledge he obtained while living here, that some Jem'Hadar existed who were capable of surviving without the white. The Vorta's search took many weeks, but when it was done, they found only four." Taran'atar lowered his collar, showing them the scar tissue where his tube had once been. "I was one.

"Odo then met with each of us. He asked us questions. He listened. In the end, he chose me to be his messenger."

"Why you?" Vaughn asked.

Taran'atar never took his eyes off Kira. "I am not certain. I think he believed that as the oldest among the four, I was somehow better suited for the task he wished to accomplish. Among my kind, I am an Honored Elder of twenty-two years as you measure them."

Taran'atar saw Kira exchange a look with Vaughn. They said nothing, and when she turned to face him again, he continued.

"I left Dominion space soon after, and had almost reached the Anomaly when my ship was attacked by others of my kind. There are some Jem'Hadar who were displeased when the war ended, who believe they needed to redeem themselves for their failure to conquer the Alpha Quadrant.

"How many?" Captain Klag interrupted, glowering at him.

"Few," Taran'atar answered. "Among us, disobedience is dealt with quickly and decisively, when detected. The Jem'Hadar follow the will of the Founders, as is the way. And they have not sanctioned any hostilities since your treaty was signed."

The Klingons didn't seem convinced, but the others visibly relaxed.

"Some of these defiant Jem'Hadar learned of my mission before they could be dealt with," Taran'atar continued. "Four strike ships attacked ours, inflicting serious damage, although we destroyed one of theirs. I was contacted by Kitana'klan when our engines failed, who wanted me to know why we had been attacked; he told me that there could never be a peace with the Alpha Quadrant until it belonged to the Dominion, and that by destroying Deep Space 9, a new war would be sparked. A war that the Dominion would win.

"Although our ship was disabled, we succeeded in repairing it enough to pursue the remaining strikers into your space. My crew fought well, but we could not defeat them all. And when I understood that we were about to be destroyed, I transported here."

Taran'atar pulled himself straighter, remembering the courage of his crew. "I would have chosen to stay with my men, who died to bring me here, but death was not my mission."

At this, both Klingon captains nodded, as if they understood. Taran'atar thought perhaps they did.

"What I found out shortly after my arrival was that Kitana'klan had also come here, with a revised plan to destroy you from within. But he knew of my presence, as well, and we remained shrouded, stalking each other as we both sought to draw attention from the station's inhabitants. But Kitana'klan was young and inexperienced. He allowed himself to be detected by the Andorian. Nevertheless, he was able to gain more time to achieve his goal by claiming the peace mission was his."

"Why didn't you reveal yourself when Kitana'klan was discovered?" Captain Picard asked.

"Because Kitana'klan did not transport to the station alone," Taran'atar responded. "Three of his crew were with him, and in the last five days, each has attempted to reach the station's fusion core. I believed my best chance to stop them was to remain shrouded, and watch for them; that is how I learned of their plans, and of Kitana'klan's deception. All three of their bodies can be found in a storage area not far from where the lower section of the station was. I can show you. I killed the last only a short time before Kitana'klan escaped. But I underestimated his abilities, arriving at the cargo bay too late . . ."

Taran'atar wasn't certain if he should ask about the Starfleet lieutenant he'd tried to help; if he had died, these people might believe he'd inadvertently caused it.

"There was a human in the bay who was bleeding to death," he said, determined to fulfill Odo's expectations of him. "A Starfleet doctor. I tried to stop the bleeding before I went in pursuit of Kitana'klan. Did he live?"

Colonel Kira spoke, for the first time since arriving. "He did."

Taran'atar nodded.

"This is a charming tale," Commander Sartai said, addressing the others, her eyes narrowed with mistrust. "But this creature has yet to offer any evidence that he is what he says he is. For all we know, the real envoy—even if we are to believe there ever was one—could be one of the three he claims to have killed. Where is the proof of his veracity?"

"Here," answered Taran'atar, retrieving from his belt the data chip. "It is from Odo. I was instructed to give it to you, so that you might share the message with others in the Alpha Quadrant."

He held it out to Kira, who made no move to take it. He could see in her eyes that she was unsure of him still. He had failed to convince her. Then he remembered the last words Odo had said to him.

"Hide nothing from them, show them you can be trusted, and only good can come from this."

Taran'atar continued to hold out the chip to her. "I tell you truthfully, Colonel Kira, I still do not understand what I am meant to achieve here, among the same aliens that defeated the Dominion. I was told understanding would come in time, and perhaps that will be so. But for now, all that matters is that a Founder has given me a mission. It is not necessary that I understand, only that I obey. Obedience brings victory. Victory is life. You may be certain that I will do as Odo has instructed me, or die in the attempt."

There was another pause, the people in the room looking at one another uncertainly. Taran'atar knew that all but a few of them had come to discuss retaliation of some kind for the attack on the station; he wondered what he would do if they went forward with those plans.

Everyone was looking at Kira Nerys now, who still hadn't taken the chip from Taran'atar's outstretched hand.

Kira reached out. She accepted the chip, looking at it with a strange expression.

"Let's see it," Admiral Ross said, and Kira handed it to him. Taran'atar found her difficult to read, but sensed a certain reluctance as she parted with the chip. She had been close with the Founder, he knew, in an emotional and physical relationship; perhaps she was angry with him for leaving her.

The admiral plugged the chip into the table's reader and they all turned to look at the viewscreen on the far wall.

15

The screen was blank—and then there was Odo, and he seemed to be gazing directly at her, the soft rumble of his voice stirring her deeply, making her throat ache with longing. Everyone else in the room ceased to matter, there was only Odo, and the way he was looking at her.

"This message is for Colonel Kira Nerys of Deep Space 9," he said briskly, but his blue eyes were gentle, the smooth curves of his face as beautiful as she remembered. Behind him, an empty room on a Dominion ship.

Oh, how I've missed you. . . .

"Nerys, I hope that you're well," he said, and she smiled a little. He must have known that she wouldn't be the only person to see his message, and was putting on what she used to call his repressed face. Direct, in control, absolutely on top of things—and beneath it, his kindness and innocence shining through like a bright light he couldn't completely veil. Perhaps she was the only one who saw it, but that only made it more personal for her . . . that she could still read him so easily, that the connection hadn't been severed.

"If you're watching this, you've most likely met Taran'atar by now," Odo said. "And he has probably explained his presence to you, but I thought you should also hear it from me.

"You know that ever since we learned how and why the Dominion had created the Jem'Hadar, I've felt a certain responsibility for what my people had done to them. Their lives have only one meaning here, to fight and die for the Founders. And because the majority of them die young, very few of them ever imagine that any other kind of existence is possible. But some do. We've all seen it.

"Among the ideas I've tried to introduce since I returned to the Link is that the Jem'Hadar deserve a chance to be freed of their dependency on ketracel-white, and to evolve without further genetic manipulation." Odo grunted, as if remembering. "You can imagine the Link's reaction to *that* suggestion."

Odo look suddenly became more intense. "I have no illusions, I know I can't transform the Jem'Hadar or the Dominion overnight. But it has to begin somewhere. My people once sent out a hundred of my kind into the galaxy to learn what they could, and to bring that knowledge home. I was one of them. It took some doing, but I convinced the Link to let me try the same thing with a single Jem'Hadar.

"I know the Jem'Hadar aren't all that popular in

the Alpha Quadrant, and with good reason, for the most part . . . but I also know that you have nothing to fear from Taran'atar. He's not dependent on white, and he never fought in the war for the Alpha Quadrant. He's there to do as you tell him, Nerys, and to experience living among different life-forms just as I did.

"My hope in sending him to you is that . . . it's a first step, a step toward change. I think you'll find him to be honest and direct, and open to new possibilities. I hope you'll let him stay for a while."

Kira glanced at Taran'atar, his emotions still too alien to be read clearly. But Kira thought she saw in his face a flicker of something she understood. Acceptance, maybe? Even hope?

"I also want to tell you," Odo went on, "and tell leaders of the Alpha Quadrant, that you have nothing to fear from the Dominion, either. The Link is also in a state of change. We've been . . . they've been considering the insights and experiences that I've brought to them, and will be for some time to come, I expect. You can believe me when I say the Dominion is closing its borders for the foreseeable future. I guess you could say I've given them a lot to think about."

Commander Sartai started to say something, and was hushed by Admiral Ross.

"We stumbled across the Dominion by accident, back before the war started," Odo said. "Most of the people from the Alpha Quadrant simply wanted to explore and to befriend those they encountered . . . and I want you to pass the message along that if the Federation and its allies want to resume that peaceful exploration, the Dominion won't interfere. I can promise you that. All the Link asks for in return is to be left alone, until it's ready to initiate contact."

Kira could feel the surprise in the room, but couldn't look away, not now. His repressed face was slipping away, the light breaking through, and he was gazing at her with love and tenderness, the look that had scared her by its intensity in the first weeks of their romance. Now, it filled her with bittersweet joy. She knew that it had been the right thing, Odo returning home to live as he was meant to live, to share with the Founders what he'd learned living among humanoids . . . and it was still the right thing, because she loved him and it was what he wanted.

"Take care, Nerys," he said, his low voice rich with sincerity and a yearning of his own, his gently passionate gaze reaching hers through tens of thousands of light-years.

He reached for something and was gone, the message delivered.

Admiral Ross sat back in his chair, as stunned as he'd been in quite some time. He looked at Colonel Kira first, but quickly looked away, seeing the barely contained emotion on her face. The personal subtext of the message was impossible to ignore, and he felt almost as though they had all invaded her privacy by watching.

The others in the room also seemed surprised, though it appeared that the news had affected each of them differently. Commander Sartai was obviously unhappy, her sharp features set in narrow lines; the Romulan government had pushed harder for the armed task force than any other, so he took her sour face as an indication that she believed Odo's message. Captains Klag and R'taga both glared at the Jem'Hadar, but with less intensity than before, and Captain Picard seemed relieved, his shoulders back, the barest possibility of a smile on his face. Commander Vaughn wore a thoughtful expression, absently stroking his carefully trimmed beard with one hand.

Kira had collected herself, and spoke first. "Is there anyone here who doesn't believe what Odo and Taran'atar told us?"

A hesitation, the powerful men and women in the room all looking to each other to see. As Ross expected, Commander Sartai answered first.

"I have strong reservations about the supposed truth of this matter," she said, the mildness of her reaction proving that she believed what she'd heard. "I wish to speak privately with the other leaders in my forces before answering."

Both Klingons were nodding, and Captain Klag spoke slowly, his voice gruff but deliberative. "We also choose to confer among ourselves."

Ross thought that both Odo and Taran'atar were telling the truth, but recognized that even if the Romulans and Klingons believed it, they would need to make a show of deciding. With the Federation leading the investigation, he knew his opinion would figure heavily in the final decision—but also that if the other Allies felt pushed, they would resist.

"Considering the evidence, I'm leaning toward Taran'atar's version of events," Ross said carefully.

"But we should all meet with our own teams to discuss this new information. Shall we reconvene here in, say, an hour's time?"

"Agreed," Klag said. Commander Sartai and the Klingon captains all stood up, nodding at Ross and at the others—when Commander Vaughn spoke up, seemingly addressing no one in particular.

"Think of it—as long as we don't bother with the Dominion, we'd be free to explore huge areas of new territory. There are unknown worlds to find, new cultures to experience . . . and just think of the untapped resources that would be available to us."

Ross held a straight face, but knew before the others left the room that Vaughn had just decided for them. The calculating gleam in Sartai's gaze, the barely hidden grins of the Klingons—the opportunities were considerable, and too important to ruin with political power plays.

And he knows it. If they weren't a hundred percent before, they are now; the investigation is as good as over.

When they were gone, Colonel Kira broke into a smile. "Well played, Commander. I'm impressed."

Vaughn smiled back at her as he stood up. "Thank you, Colonel."

"Since this is a Federation matter, and you already know where I stand on it, I'll take my leave," she said, and then nodded at Taran'atar. He'd stood silently during the exchange, still watching the blank viewscreen as if he expected Odo to reappear.

"Taran'atar, until I have a chance to explain your presence to the station, I'm going to ask you to stay in one of our guests' quarters. I'll take you to them now."

The Jem'Hadar nodded. "Shall I shroud?"

The colonel hesitated, then shook her head. "We might as well let people start getting used to the idea."

Ross didn't envy her the task of teaching a Jem'Hadar anything, but Taran'atar did seem to be different than most. He told Kira that he'd contact her as soon as the Allies returned, and she and Taran'atar left—after she took the data chip with Odo's message, tucking it into her uniform.

When the three Starfleet officers were alone, Picard turned to Vaughn with a smile. "Nicely done, Elias."

The commander accepted gracefully before turning his sharp, bright gaze to Ross. "Any doubts, Bill?"

Ross shrugged, thinking that Elias Vaughn was one of the few people below the rank of Admiral who could get away with calling him "Bill."

"Personally? No, not really. Though I have to admit, I'd feel a lot better about this if we had some way to test the Dominion's sincerity."

Vaughn smiled enigmatically. "I have a few ideas, but I have to check on a couple of things before I can commit to anything."

The commander excused himself, leaving Ross and Picard alone. They talked casually for a few more minutes about Starfleet business—the rumors about the Romulans making diplomatic overtures to the Breen, the probability of establishing a permanent Allied presence in the Bajoran sector, the mandates currently being reviewed by the Federation Council. Picard mentioned that the *Enterprise* would be leaving shortly, so as not to overtax DS9's limited power reserves . . . which in turn led him to suggest to Ross that every Federation starship in the task force supply one emergency generator to the station. That should carry them through until a permanent solution to the reactor core problem could be found.

Ross approved of the idea, and both officers agreed that Colonel Kira seemed to be handling her command well, stepping into Ben Sisko's shoes without a hitch.

Finally, Picard said he should see to his ship, and Ross decided he should put his call in to HQ . . . and when he stood up, Ross realized that he actually felt physically lighter, as if a weight had been lifted from his chest and shoulders. The nightmare of the last week was over, their journey to DS9 thankfully, mercifully unnecessary—there would be no war, no more Cardassians to mourn.

At least not today, he thought. It was enough.

Once Vaughn made it clear why he was calling, they wasted no time before bringing out their big guns—a four-way conference was quickly set up. Rear Admiral Presley, Vice Admiral Richardson, and perhaps the top mediator/negotiator for Starfleet MI, Captain Lily Shalhib, were online, three people with extraordinary careers in Starfleet . . . and security clearance similar to his own.

Vaughn listened respectfully for a good twenty minutes, faintly amused and a little flattered by how hard they were trying to talk him out of his decision. Captain Shalhib, in particular, was extremely convincing.

". . . and security risks aside, it smacks of sheer recklessness." Shalhib was saying. "Really, Elias, I think you ought to take some time to think this through. You're easily one of our best independent operatives, and that isn't something you can expect us to simply do without. . . ."

When they started to repeat themselves, Vaughn restated his intentions, making arguments of his own. "I'm more than qualified, I have the background, the diplomatic awareness, and the desire."

The nice stopped there. Vice Admiral Richardson shook his head, frowning, and Vaughn could see both Presley and Shalhib steeling themselves for what was coming.

"I'm sorry, Elias, this isn't open to discussion," Richardson said. "You're too valuable to us, especially now."

Vaughn's eyes narrowed, thinking that there wasn't a moment in his career when his superiors would *not* have said "especially now." He reminded himself that they were only doing their jobs. "Then I tender my resignation from Starfleet, effective immediately."

They all stared at him, Presley forcing a smile. "That's a joke, right?"

"Try me," Vaughn said. "I know this puts all of you in an awkward position, but let's not forget, this is my *life* we're discussing. I've made my decision. If you don't like it, I'll take my retirement instead, and go through with my plans as a civilian."

There was a pause, and then Shalhib spoke, suddenly seeming very tired.

"Will you excuse us for a moment, Commander?"

"Take your time," Vaughn said, and the split screen went to standby.

A moment later, they were back—and he knew

immediately that he wouldn't have to step down, from the reluctant surrender he saw in their eyes.

"Congratulations, Elias," Presley said. "Pending final approval from your new CO, I'll have the official order put through within a day."

Vaughn sincerely thanked each of them and signed off, unable to wipe the smile from his face.

16

After the morning staff meeting, Ro walked slowly to her office, thinking over the events of the last few days, both good and bad.

The Allied task force had agreed to stand down in the early hours of the morning, which was good news for everyone. Ro could feel the relief in the air, could see it in the faces of the people she passed. Most of the ships had already left, although a few would remain in Bajoran space, to be on hand for any other surprise visits from the Gamma Quadrant. The news that the Dominion had agreed to allow exploration on their side of the wormhole was already spreading throughout the station; Ro was cautiously optimistic about it, along with just about everyone else.

Three of her officers were dead, killed by Kitana'klan . . . who had been killed in turn by another Jem'Hadar, who would be staying on the station. Kira had assured all of them that Taran'atar was atypical, and from his actions so far, there was no argument—he'd saved Dr. Bashir's life and kept the station safe, four times over. Lieutenant Nog had strenuously objected, but after Kira played Odo's message, he'd lapsed into quiet grumbling. The colonel made it clear that she expected all of her senior staff to meet and work with Taran'atar, pointing out that the station population would be looking to them—that his being accepted would depend in large part on how the officers treated him.

Ro had to admit, she was looking forward to meeting him—because of how much she *wasn't* looking forward to tomorrow's memorial service, for the civilian tech and the deputies Kitana'klan had murdered. Wasa, Devro and Cryan had all been good young men, and she'd gladly shake the hand of the man who had taken out their killer, Jem'Hadar or no.

Ro reached the Promenade and started for her office, wondering if Yevir Linjarin was still around. Probably; the prophecy upload debacle hadn't been resolved so far as she knew, and Yevir was definitely not one to let something like that rest. She still planned on filing a report with the Ministry of Justice, but that seemed minor next to Kira's act of defiance. Ro never would have guessed that the colonel had it in her to challenge a vedek, or to choose truth over faith. She knew she was simplifying, knew that Kira still didn't entirely believe in Ohalu's prophecies, but the colonel's belief in the Bajoran people was admirable . . .

. . . though I doubt Kasidy sees it that way. Unlike the rest of Bajor, Ro didn't particularly care where Kasidy chose to live, but she sincerely wished the

woman luck; she seemed like a good person. If Ro had been in her position, she probably would have lost her mind by now.

Word was going around that Shar's mother had the Andorian seat on the Federation Council, which was kind of a surprise since he'd never mentioned it. Obviously, he hadn't wanted anyone to know. He'd been uncharacteristically subdued at the meeting, and had seemed reluctant to make eye contact, which suggested he was embarrassed, though Ro couldn't imagine why. She decided she'd seek him out later, just to make sure he was okay.

Ro was so preoccupied with the ongoing complications of life on DS9 that she was actually walking through her office door before she realized that Quark was inside, waiting for her with a steaming mug in hand. She'd been expecting a visit for a couple of days, ever since she first noticed his recently acquired habit of watching her from outside his restaurant.

"Lieutenant, good morning," he said, charmingly formal as he extended the cup to her. "Forgive my presumptuousness, but I've noted that you have a fondness for hot tea, and I've been told that this is an excellent blend. It's very expensive."

Ro paused in reaching for it. "Does that mean I have to pay for it?"

Quark looked faintly wounded. "No, no, of course not! It's a gift. Call it a token of my appreciation for your superb work with the evacuation last night. You know, you really know how to pack a crowd."

She accepted the mug and walked to her desk, smiling at him as she sat down. "Thanks, Quark, that's very considerate of you."

The bartender smiled back, bowing a little and looking up at her over his lashes. "You're welcome . . . Laren."

She sipped the tea, and nodded her approval. "This *is* good; what's it called?"

He hesitated for so long that she was about to ask him again when he suddenly blurted out, "Darjeeling, would you have dinner with me?"

Even knowing that it was coming, Ro felt her heart beat a little faster. How long had it been since someone had asked her to dinner, or looked at her the way Quark did?

"Quark . . ." Ro set her mug down, feeling a little awkward. She was terrible at romantic dealings, having never really practiced. She also actually liked Quark, and didn't want to hurt his feelings.

"Never mind," he said briskly, nodding at her, the open look of hope giving way to a half scowl. "Forget I asked."

"No, wait," she said. "Listen . . . right now I'm going through a kind of—self-evaluation period, I guess you could say, and while I'm flattered by your invitation, the truth is, I really don't want to be involved with anyone right now."

For a split second, she thought she saw disappointment—but then he was grinning, shaking his head.

"Involved? Who said anything about getting involved? I'm talking about eating together, you know, as friends."

Ro was pretty sure she knew better, but if that was how he wanted to handle it, she was willing to play along.

"Oh. In that case, yes. Not tonight, though, I'll be too tired. I've got a lot of work today. In fact, maybe we should wait a couple of days, until things calm down around here."

Quark was entirely too casual, but his eyes were gleaming. "Sure, tonight's bad for me, too. Maybe in a couple of days. Or next week, even."

"Maybe," Ro said, wondering if she'd made a mistake. He was entirely too happy for having just been turned down. "As friends, though, right?"

"Absolutely, you bet," Quark said, backing out of her office, showing most of his teeth in a sharpened grin. "Friends, got it. You won't regret this."

He was gone before she could say anything else. Ro sighed, staring down into her mug of tea, regretting it already. Oh, well; she'd made her position clear, and he'd just have to—

"May I come in?"

Ro looked up, and saw Captain Picard standing in the entrance to her office.

Ro stood up quickly, almost upsetting her tea. "Captain. Yes, of course."

He stepped into her office, standing stiffly as he looked around, and she was more than a little astonished to see him looking uncomfortable. Jean-Luc Picard was *never* uncomfortable.

"So," he said, finally looking at her. "A Bajoran Militia lieutenant, special forces, and chief security officer for the station. It's good that you're putting your tactical training to good use."

There was no spite or animosity in his voice, or in his coolly appraising gaze. Ro nodded, finding that she was still completely intimidated by the man.

"Yes, sir. The rank is honorary. I was appointed here, after the war. Recently, I mean." She mentally slapped herself, her heart pounding.

Picard nodded, still studying her face. "I see. Do you think you'll stay here?"

Again, Ro searched for the anger she expected and again, came up empty. He was simply asking. She thought about his question, thought about telling him she was fine and happy and all settled in, but found that she didn't want to lie. He hadn't come here to condemn her; this was her chance to be honest with him.

"I don't know," she said uncertainly. "I think so, but sometimes . . . sometimes I'm not sure if it's what I want."

"Commitments can be difficult," he said, nodding again. "But there are benefits to following through. You've done well for yourself; perhaps you should stay for a while."

Ro swallowed heavily, no longer able to stand it. "Captain, about what happened—" she began, and he raised one hand, silencing her.

"Everyone has regrets, Lieutenant . . . and the consequences of our actions, of the choices we make, can stay with us for a long time. I only stopped by to say that I hope you won't let your past dictate your future—and to wish you well."

Suddenly, Ro found herself perilously close to tears. She'd betrayed him . . . and it seemed that he had forgiven her.

"Thank you, Captain," she said, struggling to keep a tremor out of her voice and failing, horrified by the thought of breaking down in front of him.

Picard took pity on her. "Well. Good luck, Lieutenant."

He nodded once, then turned and walked out, straightening his uniform as he disappeared into the crowd on the Promenade.

Ro sat down, elated and weak with gratitude, depressed and uncertain of everything. She stared at her cup of tea until she felt the threat of tears pass; it was ice cold before she felt ready to move on with her day.

After saying good-bye to Colonel Kira in her office—and receiving more of her sincerely felt appreciation for the delivery of the Orb—Picard headed for the *Enterprise,* thinking that he was glad he'd gone to see Ro Laren. There had been a time when he'd felt only anger and disappointment at the thought of what she'd done; after the faith he'd placed in her, her abrupt decision to join the Maquis—and to sabotage a Starfleet operation, in the process—had been a surprise, to say the least.

Something about her had always appealed to him on some fundamental level, though he'd never been able to quantify those feelings to his satisfaction . . . and still couldn't, not really. The need for second chances, perhaps. All he knew was that when he'd seen her yesterday, when he'd seen the open self-doubt and shame in her eyes, he'd realized that he didn't want her to carry such sorrow on his behalf. It was as simple as that.

An exciting and unusual day, all in all, he thought, stepping from the pylon turbolift to head for his waiting ship. From the Orb to an evacuation, to a Jem'Hadar ambassador and the changes his presence had wrought, Picard was quite satisfied with their stop at DS9. He was sorry they couldn't stay longer, but the ship needed a more extensive maintenance than DS9 could currently provide; Starbase 375 wasn't too far away, and the crew still needed to stretch their legs. He thought they might stay there for two or three days, let everyone take a few deep breaths before they continued on with Starfleet business. . . .

"Captain, would you mind if I walked you to the bridge?"

Vaughn was standing just inside the outer docking ring, smiling. Picard shook his head, glad to see him; he'd planned on asking the commander to come to the ship before they disembarked, knowing that Will and Deanna, at least, would want a chance to say good-bye. And he was to know if his suspicions about Vaughn's future were correct.

"Not at all," he said, and the two men stepped on to the ship, heading for the turbolift. They stood side by side, speaking without look at each other as the lift ascended to the bridge. "I suppose you know what I did," Vaughn said.

Picard smiled. "I had my suspicions," he admitted, "especially once you mentioned having ideas about testing the Dominion's sincerity. This puts you in quite an extraordinary position, Elias. You'll be taking point in the renewed exploration of the Gamma Quadrant, if Starfleet approves it."

Vaughn grinned. "Hell, even if they don't approve it," he said, as the lift halted and its doors opened.

They strode together to the center of the bridge, Geordi reporting from the aft engineering station that the *Enterprise* was in good shape for their trip. All of the senior staff was present, and when Vaughn revealed his plans, the reception was overwhelmingly positive. Even Data turned on his emotions just for the experience; he put on a grin and warmly shook Vaughn's hand, congratulating him heartily. Elias Vaughn had obviously made an impression on the crew that wouldn't soon be forgotten.

After Deanna had embraced Vaughn, promising to keep in touch, only Picard was left to bid the commander farewell. They walked back up to the turbolift together, neither speaking until they reached the doors.

Picard smiled, extending his hand. "It's been a pleasure, Elias. I sincerely hope we'll have an opportunity to work together again."

Vaughn reached out to clasp Picard's hand with both of his own. "As do I. Jean-Luc, thank you for everything."

"You're welcome, sir."

With a final grin, the commander stepped onto the lift and the doors closed, taking him to his future. Picard went to his chair, and Will began the process of leading them away from Deep Space 9, communications calling ops, Data laying in a course for Starbase 375.

A remarkable man, the commander; Picard decided he'd have to make a point of bringing the *Enterprise* back this way in a year or so, time and circumstances allowing. Elias, Ro, the colonel, Taran'atar; it would be interesting to see what developed.

"Take us out," Riker said, and Picard leaned back in his chair, wishing he'd taken Elias horseback riding, deciding that he would indulge himself soon after they were under way; life was too short not to take full advantage.

After Picard left Kira's office, she decided that it was time to reveal the Orb to Vedek Capril. With all that had happened since the captain had presented it to her, there'd been no opportunity—and though she'd wanted to track down Shakaar and tell him first, she now thought that it might be best to let the station's vedeks handle the revelation. Her plate was full enough without having to manage the fervor that a returned Orb would create.

Kira stepped off the lift onto the Promenade, and headed straight for the shrine. She could hardly wait to see Vedek Capril's reaction, or Vedek Po's, or that of the ranjens who assisted them. The Orb, Kira was certain, would bring some much-needed harmony to her people, as a sign that the Prophets were still with them.

An account from the Bajoran Chamber of Ministers had come in just before Picard had stopped by, reporting that mass gatherings were being held all over the planet, confused and worried citizens meeting to talk about Ohalu's book. It had been fourteen hours since she'd uploaded it, and although the prophecies had apparently stirred up plenty of unrest, no one was panicking, or rioting in the streets, contrary to Yevir's assertion. A new dialogue had been created, that was all, and Kira believed that the returned Orb would ease any turmoil in that dialogue. She was grateful to the Prophets for allowing the Orb to be found and brought back to Bajor; it was one of the few bright lights in days of darkness, along with the message from Odo. . . .

Kira wasn't ready to let Odo in, not quite yet. The feelings were simple but the thoughts weren't, and she'd have plenty of time to miss him in the days to come, after the station was repaired and its population was at rest. She pushed the image of his well-loved face out of her mind, thinking instead of Taran'atar, of how to introduce him to the station—

"Nerys."

Kasidy was standing near the doors of the temple, her arms crossed, her shoulders hunched with tension. Kira looked around, and saw that a number of Bajorans had stopped in the middle of the Promenade, talking to one another softly as they stared at Kas. Kira felt herself flush with guilt, and hurriedly stepped into the temple, beckoning for Kas to join her.

The shrine was empty and quiet, the attendants apparently all in the back offices, the lights low. Kira turned, looking into Kasidy's face, and saw a careful guardedness in her usually mild brown eyes, a caution that had never been there before. Knowing that it was her fault made Kira's heart ache.

"Kas, I . . . I'm so sorry," she said, wondering if she'd ever be able to make it up her.

Kasidy nodded. She didn't seem angry so much as resigned, which was much worse.

"You did what you had to do," Kas said calmly. "I wish you hadn't, but I understand why. I might have done the same thing myself, if I were you."

Kira shook her head. "If I'd known what this would do to you, I would have thought twice," she said, hoping that Kasidy believed at least that much.

"But all of this will go away, I promise, and sooner than you think. The people of Bajor care about you, Kas, they're not going to turn your life into some kind of a . . . a religious attraction."

"You're right," Kas said, still calm and matter-of-fact. "Because I'm going to Earth, to be with Jake and Joseph, at least for the duration of my pregnancy. I'll be leaving day after tomorrow . . . and I may not be coming back. I don't know yet."

Kira felt her stomach clench, a rush of desperation and denial moving like heat throughout her body. "Kasidy, no! Your house is finished, and all of your friends are here—please, please don't go, not because of what I did. What can I do, how can I fix this?"

Kasidy reached out and touched Kira lightly on the arm. "I don't blame you, and you shouldn't blame yourself. It's just—I woke up this morning to find something like eleven thousand messages posted to me, on the communications net. I read about fifty of them, but it was enough—Nerys, some of those people were offering to *die* for me, to be part of the sacrifice for the Avatar. For my *baby*."

Kira felt sick. "Oh, Kas, I'm so sorry. I'm sure that it's just a few people . . ."

She trailed off, realizing that it wouldn't make a difference. Even one was too many.

Kasidy smiled faintly. "It's okay. I wish I could stay, but I just can't handle this kind of stress, not now. My body can't handle it. This is for the best. And maybe I will come back, once things die down a little."

Stricken by the hollowness of the statement, Kira

searched for something else she could say, something to make things right again, but she was grasping at air. Kasidy gave her arm a squeeze before turning and walking out, leaving Kira alone.

Kira sat down on the back bench, closed her eyes, and started to pray.

17

Commander Vaughn found Kira in the Bajoran shrine just off the Promenade. When he stepped into the temple's entrance, he didn't see her at first, and wondered if the computer had steered him wrong. The shrine itself was lovely, the complete lack of ornate or lavish trappings adding to the atmosphere of faith and good feelings. A light scent of incense and candle wax lingered in the still air.

Vaughn took a few more steps inside and saw the colonel, sitting on the back pew to the far left, where she'd been blocked from sight by the entrance wall. Her eyes were closed, and he realized she was meditating or praying, her still face tilted upward slightly. Not wanting to interrupt, Vaughn started to back quietly out of the room, thinking that he could approach her about the XO position later.

Kira opened her eyes, turning to look at him. Her

features were relaxed, but somehow not serene, as though she'd just woken from an unhappy dream.

"Hello, Commander."

Vaughn smiled. "Sorry to interrupt—perhaps we could meet when you're finished . . .?"

"That's all right," she said, pushing a lock of hair behind her ear. "I'm having a little trouble concentrating, anyway. Have a seat."

Vaughn sat down, shifting around to face her, wondering what was wrong. She definitely seemed tense, and perhaps a little sad. Kira didn't strike him as someone who would be comfortable sharing her emotions with a virtual stranger, so he didn't ask.

"I never got a chance to thank you, for what you did last night," she said. "If you hadn't been there, a lot of people would have died. You were instrumental in saving the station."

"I really just helped *you* save it," he said, and took a deep breath. "Though as long as you're thinking well of me, how would you feel about keeping me around? I noticed you have an opening for an executive officer, and I'd very much like to fill it."

Kira hesitated, then slowly nodded, smiling a little. "That would be great, assuming Starfleet is agreeable. . . . You're overqualified for the position, if you don't mind me saying."

Vaughn grinned, feeling as though the last piece of a puzzle was fitting into place. "I've already worked that out, actually. My, ah, superiors have agreed to it, as long as you're not opposed to the appointment."

Kira looked a bit puzzled. "I was under the impression that your background is primarily tactical. . . ."

"It is," Vaughn said. "But I had an experience recently that made me want to try something else. An Orb experience, actually."

Kira's eyes widened. "Captain Picard told me you found the Orb, I can't believe I forgot to thank you—you have no idea how much this means to my people."

"Actually, maybe I do, a little," Vaughn said, smiling. "Did the captain tell you that when we found it, the ark was open? Everyone on the away team was affected. For me, it was . . . it changed me. It made me realize that I didn't want to be doing what I was doing, which is a big part of why I want to be your second."

Kira was nodding, a look of real understanding on her face. It was a look that made Vaughn feel safe to tell it all, a look that told him she knew the power of the experience.

"I don't want to fight anymore, Colonel," Vaughn said. "I want to be here. I want to be a part of the changes that are happening, here and now. When I was on that freighter, remembering who I once wanted to be, reliving experiences that I worked so hard to forget . . . I saw that it wasn't too late for me."

"The Orb was on a freighter?" Kira asked. "A Cardassian freighter?"

Something in her tone gave Vaughn pause. "That's right," he said. "The *Kamal.* It was trapped in a conflicted energy mass, had been for it least three decades."

"Were there Bajorans on board?" The look on Kira's face told him that she was more than simply curious.

"Yes."

"Did you . . ." Kira took a deep breath and blew it out. Her expression was almost fearful.

No, not fearful. Awed.

"Did you find the Orb in a cargo bay? With Bajorans and Cardassians?"

Vaughn nodded, wondering if Picard had mentioned it, knowing already that he hadn't. "Yes."

"I dreamed it," Kira said wonderingly. "The day that the Jem'Hadar attacked the station. I dreamed that I was in a lost freighter, in a cargo bay. And all around me were Bajoran refugees, and their captors, and they were dying—"

"—asphyxiating," Vaughn said.

"—and there was a light in the back of the bay—"

"—and Benjamin Sisko was there," Vaughn said, taking a chance. He hadn't told anyone else, but she knew already, not a trace of surprise on her face as she nodded.

They stared at one another, Vaughn not sure what it meant, not sure that he had to know. He remembered telling Jean-Luc only a day before that strange things happened, things that might never be explained.

There might never be an answer to how it had happened, but Vaughn thought he knew why.

"I was meant to find it, and bring it to you," he said, knowing that he couldn't back it up, that there was no proof beyond the dream of one woman and the exceptional experience of one man. It didn't matter. It was true, and Kira knew it as well as he did.

"Welcome to Deep Space 9, Commander," Kira said softly, and although he hadn't been assigned quarters, hadn't even seen a quarter of the station or met more than a handful of people, Vaughn thought that he was probably home at last.

* * *

When she was alone again, having sent Vaughn to ops to introduce himself around, to find quarters and get situated, Kira went to the private room where the Orb of Prophecy and Change sat on its low pedestal. She closed the door behind her and went to the storage cabinet where the Orb of Memory was hidden, still waiting to be given back to the people.

Kira gently lifted the precious ark out of the cabinet and placed it on the floor, kneeling in front of it. The Prophets had been trying to tell her something, all along, and she hadn't understood—but she understood now. Vaughn was right; he'd been meant to find the Orb, and she'd been meant to receive it. And the only way for her to find out *why* was to open the ark, to let the Prophets speak to her, if They saw fit.

She closed her eyes for a moment, silently reciting a prayer of thanks for all of the gifts They gave, and opened the ark, the beautiful light of the Prophets filling the room, the room disappearing until there was only Their will, Their strength.

18

Yevir had stayed in his quarters since returning from the aborted evacuation. He wouldn't be able to get a shuttle seat for another day—departures to Bajor had been cut in half because of the fuel shortages—so he spent a fair amount of time doing what he could to manage the situation from the station.

He spoke with Vedeks Eran and Frith, who had already called for a full Assembly meeting, to discuss how best to handle the crisis. Over the next few days, Eran said, they expected hundreds of vedeks to travel to the Assembly hall, to collaborate on an official assertion of denouncement. The book of lies had already been publicly condemned by the Assembly, of course, but it would take more than a simple statement to silence the public outcry. Yevir wondered how long it would be before the first Ohalu cults sprang up, growing from the disease like poisonous flowers.

And all because of Kira Nerys.

The thought of Nerys's incredible, terrible act had made sleep impossible, and prayer nearly so. Yevir had spent much of the night pacing his rooms, unable to concentrate on his love for the Prophets, to find solace in Their embrace. He tried to console himself with thoughts of petitioning to take her command away, perhaps even finding a way to force her to leave Bajor, but it didn't help him find peace. The damage had been done, out of blindness or malice, he couldn't be sure, but he knew that guiding Bajor through the resulting spiritual chaos might very well take years.

Which was why, when the companel in his room chimed, the last person he expected it to be was Kira Nerys, speaking without a trace of apology, not even a hint of shame. If he needed any more proof that there was something wrong with her, the obvious self-satisfaction in her voice was it.

"Vedek Yevir, would you come to runabout pad C, as soon as possible? You might want to bring your things with you, too. We're going to Bajor."

She commed off before he could ask any questions.

Yevir considered ignoring her request, but returning to Bajor as quickly as possible was in the best interests of the people . . . and to be truthful with himself, he was afraid that he wouldn't be able to find forgiveness for Kira.

When he'd turned his life over to the Prophets, he'd let go of anger and prejudice and malignity, leaving behind those things that separated him from Their light. He knew he was only mortal, but Their Touch, through the Emissary, had relieved him of pessimism and negativity. His heart had been opened to greater things . . .

. . . but how do I forgive such a staggering disdain for faith, for the Prophets themselves?

He didn't know. What he did know was that he didn't want to wait another day to return home; the Assembly needed him, they needed a strong hand to lead, so that they could lead others. He quickly gathered his things and headed for the bay, wondering why Kira wanted to go to Bajor. She'd already created havoc enough, even insulting the Emissary's wife with her blasphemous designs . . .

. . . which was why he was surprised when he stepped into the runabout airlock and saw Kasidy Yates standing with Kira, near the runabout *Euphrates*. Ro Laren was also there, just inside the ship's entrance.

"Ready to go," Ro said.

Yevir slowly walked toward them, not sure what to expect—and saw that Kasidy and Ro both wore similar expressions of uncertainty. Only Kira seemed to understand what was happening, and as he drew closer, he was shocked to see the light that emanated from her, the blazing eyes and tranquil demeanor of one who has recently been with the Prophets.

How can that be? It didn't seem possible, but the effects of an Orb experience or vision were unmistakable. Her *pagh* radiated both strength and placidity, her gaze on fire with comprehension.

When he reached the trio of women, Kira smiled at him. "I'm glad you decided to join us, Linjarin."

"What's this about?" he asked curtly, not at all sure he liked what he was seeing. How could They speak to her, after what she'd done?

The Prophets are wise in all things, he hastily amended. It wasn't for him to question.

"Funny you should ask," Kira said, still smiling. "Because I'm not really sure myself. We're going to B'hala, I know that much . . . and I believe I'll know what to do when we get there."

Yevir nodded, knowing that sometimes it was like that, still not quite understanding why They'd chosen her—and he realized that his concerns about finding forgiveness for Kira Nerys weren't about his *capacity* for that forgiveness . . . it was about his desire. Prophets help him, he didn't want to see her absolved, because she didn't deserve it.

"Shall we?" Kira asked, lit from within by awareness.

Ro and Kasidy turned and walked to the open hatch, and clutching his bag, Yevir reluctantly followed.

After the strained and silent journey to Bajor—except for Colonel Kira, who was perfectly content to sit smiling to herself—Ro was more than ready to get off the runabout. Yevir had been relentlessly moody, stalking around the *Euphrates* like a troubled child, pausing occasionally to gaze at Kasidy with adoring eyes. Kasidy had ignored him entirely, only holding herself and exuding a kind of soft sadness. Ro normally didn't mind avoiding conversation, but the atmosphere had been strangely tiring, and when they finally arrived, she was the first one on the transporter pad.

When they materialized at B'hala, in a clear-front office near the top of the city, Ro was amazed at just how huge the dig actually was—before them stretched a vast pit, filled with levels and layers of unearthed ruins, those at the very bottom so far away that it felt like they were standing in front of an optical illusion.

I had no idea it was so . . . beautiful. Religious significance aside, the crumbling city was magnificent to behold, speaking to the longevity and tenacity of Bajoran culture. The afternoon sun spread across the city in long shadows, dappling all of it in lovely, random patterns of light.

While Kira spent a few minutes talking with someone who worked at Site Extension, whatever that was, Ro gazed down at the ancient buildings and spires, her hands pressed to the cool window. Kasidy and Yevir stood on either side of her, also looking down, expressionless. Ro wasn't sure exactly what Kira was planning, but decided she was glad she'd come along, if only to have seen such an eternal and glorious thing in her lifetime.

When Kira rejoined them, she carried four light sticks and a small rock hammer. She seemed to have come down a little from whatever Orb high she'd been on, but she was still glowing too much for Yevir's taste, Ro could see it in the set of his jaw.

"What now?" Kasidy asked quietly, as Kira passed out the lights.

"Now we transport to where the book was found," Kira said.

"Why?" Yevir asked, still endeavoring to wear his pious serenity like some kind of armor. "And why the hammer? B'hala is sacred ground, it's not open to anyone who feels like participating in the dig."

Kira smiled, shrugging. "I still don't know why,

exactly. All I know is that there's an answer here, close to where Reyla found the book."

Kira gave the coordinates to the young ranjen who was operating the transporter, clicking on her light stick as they returned to the pad. Ro did the same—

—and was glad she had, when they materialized in a small, dark place a second later, underground cold, the air suffused with the smell of age and dust.

As Kas and Yevir turned on their lights, Ro saw that they were in a small room, empty except for a long, low shelf made of stone, a few broken clay pots—and an open space at the base of the far wall, where someone had recently been excavating.

"That's where she found it," Kira said, her voice hollow in the empty air. Yevir actually shuddered before turning away.

"Come this way," Kira said, walking to the uneven arch that marked the entrance to the room. There was a corridor past the arch, obviously newly unearthed, great piles of dusty, untouched stones randomly strewn throughout.

They walked in a line behind her, Ro bringing up the rear, nervously wondering how far down they were and where Kira was leading them. The darkness was oppressive, swallowing the light, a total blackness reclaiming the ground as they walked on. For some reason, Ro felt very small, as though they were a line of tiny insects crawling through a universe of tunnel.

Finally, the meandering corridor stopped, a dead end of fragile-looking stackstone, the slaty layers eroded by tens of thousands of years. Kira stopped, turning to face them. Her face was eerily lit by the glow of the sticks, her eyes like dark holes.

"Here," she said, almost in a whisper, handing her light stick to Ro. "This is as far as they've dug down; we're at the very bottom of B'hala's very lowest level. The farthest from the city's center, too."

"Do you know why yet?" Kasidy asked, also keeping her voice low. It somehow seemed obligatory, not to speak too loud in such a deep, dark place.

"I think so," Kira said. "It's about you, Kas. And about the book, and your baby."

Without another word, Kira turned and struck the face of the dead-end wall with the rock hammer, the *chink* of the stone being hit somehow not as loud as Ro would have expected. Layers of gray stackstone, pitted and brittle, fell at Kira's feet as she pounded the wall twice, three times, a fourth—

—and on her fifth strike, she broke through into an open space, the sound of the hammer disappearing into a seeming abyss beyond the wall.

Kira dropped the tool and pulled at the ragged edges of the hole with both hands, the brittle rock coming off in plates. In only a minute or two, she had opened a space large enough to step through.

"What is this?" Yevir asked, not so haughty in the darkness, his voice hushed.

"Let's see," Kira said, still smiling. She took her light stick back from Ro, turned, and stepped through the opening, leaving them no real choice but to follow—Kasidy first, then Yevir, awkwardly pulling at his robes, and finally Ro.

Kira held up her light as soon as she stepped through, seeing the place that the Prophets had led her . . . and the full understanding of her Orb experience came into her grasp, the information They'd secreted in her mind moving into her awareness.

In front of her and to either side, stretching away for kilometers, she knew, were corridors upon corridors of rough-hewn crypts, natural and created, openings in the rock where thousands of bodies—ten thousand—had gently mummified or decayed to dust, millennia ago. Each had been sealed by cairns of stone, each closed space undisturbed by time or the elements.

Behind her, Kasidy drew a sharp breath. Yevir said nothing. It was Ro who broke the silence, holding out her light stick, her voice a rough whisper in the echoing dark.

"The prophecy of the ten thousand," she said, and Kira nodded, walking toward the nearest crypt-riddled wall, the truth spilling out as it reached her conscious mind.

"These are the remains of the men and women who kept Ohalu's book safe," she said, her light shining down on hundreds of carefully placed rocks, just for the crypts that were closest. She knew that each individual tomb throughout the extensive network had been sealed the same way, a testament to the binding strengths of their convictions. "They were brought here one by one and in groups, through the centuries, all long before B'hala was lost. Ten thousand of them."

"So many . . ." Yevir said, a thread of discouragement in his soft voice. Kira didn't know if his despair came from the vast number of "diseased" Bajorans, or the realization that the supposedly profane prophecy was true. Nor did she care; Yevir would have to find his own peace with it.

"Despite the prevailing orthodoxy that sought to suppress it, all of these people knew that Ohalu had been Touched," Kira said. "They refused to hide from the truth, that the Prophets could also be experienced as teachers—and they protected the book, because of the prophecy of the Avatar."

She turned to Kasidy, smiling at the absolute wonder—and relief—on her face. "They lived and died for the hope that the birth of your child would one day represent the promise of a new age for Bajor. The birth itself will be a catalyst of a kind . . . but your baby will be your own, Kas, not some symbol, or representation. You don't have anything to fear."

Even as she was speaking, Kasidy walked toward the beginning of the corridor to their left, raising her light stick. There was an opening in the wall that hadn't been sealed, a pile of rocks on the ground next to it.

"Why is that one empty?" Yevir asked tonelessly.

Kira knew, not sure if the final clarity came from the Prophets or her own understanding—but it was Kas who answered, turning back to look at Yevir, wearing the tiniest curve of a smile.

"It's for the last guardian of the book," she said. "It's for Istani Reyla."

19

Vedek Yevir Linjarin walked to the center of the small stage, holding his head high. Nearly everyone on Bajor would be watching, he knew, and it was important for them to see that their spiritual leaders had not lost their dignity or their poise.

Yevir ignored the recording cameras aimed at the podium, instead addressing the vedeks and ranjens who had gathered at the indoor arena, placing his hands on the pulpit and gazing up into their ranks. Hundreds of them, yet it was so silent, he imagined that they could hear the beating of his own heart.

Only the truth. The Prophets deserve no less.

"Only two days ago, an unacknowledged book of prophecy was uploaded into Bajor's communications network, anonymously," he began, his voice carrying through the room. A strong voice; the voice of a leader.

"The Vedek Assembly had heard of the book, but until it was placed in the public domain, none of us had read it—and I must admit, some of us were afraid . . . at first. Afraid that the Prophets would somehow be overlooked in the controversy that was inspired; afraid, perhaps, of the Bajoran people finding out that we knew of this book, but had never spoken of it."

Nods from the assembled now, as they heard and acknowledged him.

"I want everyone to know, to understand—it was I who pushed for this book to be condemned," he said, finding strength in sharing his awareness of his faults. "I was afraid, because I looked away from the Prophets. Because for a moment, I forgot how strong, how open the Bajoran people are. I forgot that we have always looked for the truth, no matter what form it takes, and that the Prophets would never—*never*—send us anything we couldn't learn to accept. The Prophets love us; we are Their children."

He could feel himself gaining momentum, could feel it reflected back at him by the men and women watching. His words held power, because they were the truth.

"I was afraid because of my own lack of faith in Them. For all of the boundless love and respect I feel for Them, I followed my first inclination—to protect Them from secular thoughts, from secular ideas. To my shame, I didn't want the Vedek Assembly's authority to be challenged, because I thought that meant some people might turn away from us—and in turning away from us, that they would turn away from the Prophets. I was wrong. I was unworthy."

Hundreds of faces frowning, shaking their heads in disagreement.

"I might have continued on my narrow path, if not for the miraculous return yesterday of the Orb of Memory," he said, wording carefully now. "The Orb, which showed us the truth of the book's final prophecy—the prophecy of the Avatar, the Emissary's child, who is not yet born."

Slow, lingering smiles of faith throughout the rows, gazes filled with the knowledge of miracles.

"The Orb has come back to us . . . and I stand before you today to address the meaning of its return, as I see it. People are beginning to criticize the unyielding stoicism, the elitist conservatism that the Assembly has come to represent to so many of you. People are expressing interest in philosophical debate, in new interpretations of truth . . . and what *I* believe is that the Orb stands for more than the Prophets' love. I believe that it's also a sign, a sign that the Prophets choose for us to be open to change. They want us to look into our pasts, to learn from our experiences, and to use our collective knowledge to rise to the challenges of our future."

A low murmur of assent rose from the assembled. Yevir felt humility in the face of such understanding, he felt their trust in him grow as he revealed his mortal flaws. It was right and true, that he should lead the revolution for change, that the Prophets had ordained. Why else had They sent him to DS9? It had all been destined from the start.

"I know it may seem strange, that I would want

to tear down the very system that has allowed me this voice, that has made it possible for me to stand here, telling you what I believe," he said. "And I'm not saying it *should* be torn down. All I mean to say is that like all of you, I am here to serve the will of the Prophets—and those among us who turn away from Their light have no place in the Bajor of tomorrow, because our lives and our world, our changing views and our established tenets, everything we do, we do for Them. It is all part of Their loving plan for us."

Yevir smiled, nodding humbly. "Thank you for listening. Walk with the Prophets."

Acceptance flowed from them like water, enveloping him in warmth and forgiveness. Yevir closed his eyes for just a second, knowing that he had reached millions of people the world over, knowing that the Prophets, too, were watching; praise be.

"What a load," Quark grumbled, turning away from the viewscreen. Morn nodded, raising his glass to the observation. At least Kai Winn hadn't hidden her insatiable craving for power; Yevir Linjarin was apparently going for some kind of humility award for *that* little performance, but it had MEGALOMANIAC written all over it. Either that, or he was a serious fanatic; either way, Bajor was in for a ride.

Quark wouldn't have bothered watching, except he knew that practically every Bajoran on the station had been permafixed to their monitors for the duration of the much-heralded speech—and it always paid to know what the zealot faction was up to. Besides, he'd already stopped taking bets on Yevir for kai, and was interested to see the man in action. From the looks of things, the only way he could lose now would be if he got caught beating up children, or delivering a sermon in the nude, something like that.

Morn was starting to get sloppy, talking about how much hair Linjarin had, so Quark casually moved to the other end of the bar, to better indulge one of his two new favorite pastimes: thinking about his impending dinner with Ro. The other was fantasizing about Shar's mother visiting the station and asking for Quark's advice on the Alpha Quadrant's economy—just as exciting, but nowhere near as immediate.

He'd already decided to take Ro to a holosuite, and to wear the new coat he'd special-ordered—off-the-rack was for losers, at least when it came to impressing the ladies; it was one of the very few expenses that he didn't skimp on, often—but he was still debating the perfect environment. He didn't want to be too obvious, so the sex palace program was definitely out . . . but maybe the harem room, minus the harem. Lots of pillows, and plenty of that veil-y fabric hanging all over the place. They could eat toasted tubeworms and drink sweet *p'losie* wine—he had a case of the stuff that was about to turn—a little conversation, a little music . . . she said she didn't want any "involvement," but Quark was a romantic at heart; he'd wear her down. He'd woo her until she couldn't think straight.

He had just formed a perfect mental picture of her in one of those teeny little harem outfits, all delicate and wispy except for a pair of gravity boots and an intimidating sneer, when the bar's companel signaled. His daydream dissolved into Morn's sloppy face, which happened to be in the way of Quark's unseeing gaze. Talk about a lobe shriveler.

Scowling, Quark smacked the panel with one fist. "What?"

"You get more and more charming every day," Kira said, her voice dripping sarcasm.

Quark made a face. "Sorry, Colonel. What?"

"I want to have a senior staff gathering tonight, in the meeting hall across from the jeweler's. Kind of an impromptu welcome for Commander Vaughn and Taran'atar."

Quark backpedaled like mad. "What a wonderful idea! Colonel, I have to say, you're . . . well, just so generous when it comes to showing your staff how much they mean to you," he marveled, throwing his heart into it. "But you know, if you really wanted to make them feel like a part of our small, close-knit community, you'd have your party *here,* where everyone could join in. You know, so that our new friends can really get to know the people they'll be living and working with every single day—"

"Drinks and appetizers for, say, fifteen people, for two hours, 2100 on," Kira snapped. "Make it nice and I'll see that you get an extra hour of computer time every day this week."

"You're such a good person, Colonel, I mean that," Quark said, but Kira commed off before he could push the dessert option. Too bad, but the extra time was incentive enough; he'd been having to run the holosuites off his own reserves, which didn't come cheap, and Kira had flat-out refused to reimburse him for the expense. As if she *hadn't* been the one who'd authorized dumping the station's entire fusion core. . . .

Ro was senior staff.

"Grimp!" Quark screamed, the server nearly dropping a tray of glasses at the sound of his own name. Worthless slug.

As Grimp scurried toward the bar, Quark made a mental list of what needed to be done to get ready for the party—and after a discreet sniff, he added taking a shower, or at least splashing some of that special cologne on, the stuff that all the dabo girls had commented on. He remembered that even Leeta had been impressed, telling him that she'd never smelled anything quite like it—

At the other end of the bar, Morn let out a huge, gaseous belch and blinked his watery eyes, his upper body weaving back and forth as if in a strong wind. Quark shook his head, wondering how it was that some people managed to get along without even a shred of class or culture.

Some things, even latinum couldn't buy. . . .

Once they reached the meeting hall, Taran'atar stayed near the door, wondering if he was supposed to approach any of the assembled. There were only six others besides himself—Kira and Vaughn, Dr. Bashir and a female Trill, and a Starfleet tactical lieutenant. The sixth was a Ferengi, bearing plates of food and drink. On the way from his quarters, the colonel had suggested that he just be himself, but that meant not speaking unnecessarily; he wanted to follow orders, but after watching the gathering for a short time period, he saw that talking to others seemed to be the purpose.

Still, Taran'atar was unsure of the appropriate action. Colonel Kira had officially announced his presence to DS9's population hours ago, but had explained to him afterward that it might be some time before he was "accepted." He didn't understand how that could be—what was there to accept? He was on the station; it was a fact. Perhaps she had been speaking figuratively—

Two people were approaching, Dr. Bashir and the Trill. They smiled, and were touching hands as they walked. Taran'atar prepared for the confrontation; he was to be himself. They stopped in front of him, and he saw that Dr. Bashir carried a small plate holding slices of unknown fruit.

"Taran'atar, I'm Ezri Dax," the Trill said, her smile fading as she looked up at him. "I want to welcome you here."

Taran'atar nodded, accepting her statement.

Bashir was also serious now, properly establishing sincerity just as the woman had. "Taran'atar, I just wanted to say again that, ah, I'm grateful to you for saving my life."

"You owe me nothing," Taran'atar said firmly, recognizing the burden of obligation Bashir had expressed. This was going well, their interchange.

"Come with us," Dax said. "We can help you interact with the others. If that's your choice."

Taran'atar nodded again, remembering what Kira had said at the meeting of his explanation. An expression of appreciation. "Thank you."

The doctor and the Trill exchanged a look, and

then both were smiling again. Taran'atar hoped he had spoken appropriately. Never in all his years had he felt so lost, so far away from the reality he understood best, but he would learn. Odo had singled him out, had spoken his name; Taran'atar would watch and learn, or, as he vowed to Kira Nerys, he would die in the attempt.

Shar joined the party a few minutes late, wishing that the colonel had been less adamant about attendance. Since the call from Charivretha, he'd spent his off-duty hours alone in his quarters, aware that his parentage had become common knowledge; he didn't want to talk about it, and had begun to avoid social interaction.

Before he'd taken a single step into the room, Quark was at his side, holding up a tray of vegetable pieces. A strange odor surrounded him, though Shar didn't know if it was the vegetables or Quark himself.

"Shar! I'm so glad you could make it, I haven't seen you around for a couple of days. Try these—fresh Bajoran vegetables, marinated in *p'losie* wine. Exquisite, don't you think?"

Shar nervously took a piece and tasted it, aware that Quark was one of those who would be treating him differently since learning about *Zhavey.* "Very good. Do you know if Nog is coming, or Lieutenant Ro?"

"Of course! Are you kidding? They're both your friends, right? Nog is a wonderful boy, I'm just thrilled that the two of you have become so close. Any friend of his, you know? And Ro . . ."

Quark grinned, lowering his voice slightly, speaking in a conspiratorial way. "Why do you think I'm wearing this cologne? It cost me a pretty strip, I don't just put it on for no good reason. What do you think?"

It smelled vaguely like deuterium fumes on a hot day, mixed with something organic and possibly decomposing.

"I've never smelled anything like it," Shar said honestly, and Quark nodded happily.

"Exactly. Say, as long as we're talking, I've been meaning to ask you—I had this really incredible idea about establishing new shipping lanes into the Beta Quadrant, and—"

"Hey, Shar."

Shar turned, grateful for the interruption. It was Nog, just arriving.

"Nephew, how nice," Quark said through a gritted smile. "I think Colonel Kira wanted to see you about something. . . ."

Nog pointed across the room. "Look, Lieutenant Bowers is holding an empty glass. You're not catering for a flat fee, are you?"

Quark hesitated, then grinned at Shar again. "If you'll excuse me . . . perhaps we can pick this up again later."

Shar put on a smile for Nog as Quark swept away. "Hello, Nog."

"You'll have to excuse my uncle," Nog said, smiling back. "He thinks that if he can get in good with you, he'll have an inside line to the Federation Council."

Shar felt that too-familiar ache inside, his heart growing heavy and sinking, but Nog wasn't finished.

"Like anyone cares who your mom is. My dad's

the Grand Nagus of Ferenginar, but what does that say about me? Nothing, that's what."

Shar blinked, looking into Nog's earnest face—and felt something starting to loosen inside.

"You don't care . . ."

"About your mother?" Nog asked. "Why would I? I don't know her."

Nog abruptly narrowed his eyes, looking across the room to where the Jem'Hadar was standing with Dr. Bashir and Ezri, the three of them talking to Commander Vaughn.

"Have you met him yet?" Nog asked.

Shar shook his head, still feeling that sense of release in his chest, feeling good for the first time since *Zhavey* had called. It didn't resolve the big problem, about what he was going to do—but if Nog didn't care about Charivretha zh'Thane . . . perhaps there were others who didn't, either.

"Well, Kira can make me talk to him, but she can't make me like it," Nog said. "And if he didn't have Odo vouching for him, I would have put in for transfer already."

"You respect Odo," Shar said.

Nog nodded. "Yeah, I guess I do. He scared me when I was younger, always checking up on me . . . but he treated me okay once I grew up a little . . ."

He trailed off, staring at Taran'atar, then looked back at Shar, visibly brightening. "So, I guess we're going to be working together for a while, on the *Defiant.* Kira says that they are going to be refitting it for two science labs, biochem and stellar cartography. It's going to take *weeks* to get everything up and running. Ensign Tenmei is supposed to drop by later, so we can start talking about the new navigation-sensor patch."

Shar nodded, wondering if he would still be on the station when it was all finished, hoping very much that he would.

"What do you think they will do about the station's fusion core?"

Nog broke into a grin. "I can't believe I forgot to tell you—I think I have the solution! I just need to make sure the numbers work, but if they do, and if I can convince the colonel to let me go ahead with it, our power problems will be over in a week!"

Shar was skeptical. "A week."

"Two, tops," Nog guaranteed. "Come on, let's go get a couple of drinks, and I'll tell you all about it."

When finally Julian got back with their drinks—Quark had run out of synthale, and dashed off to the bar to get more—Ezri and Vaughn were smiling at one another like old friends, Vaughn nodding and shaking her hand.

Julian handed Ezri her drink and Vaughn excused himself, taking Taran'atar with him to meet Lieutenant Bowers. Ezri was glowing.

"I take it your conversation went poorly," Julian said, smiling. Across the room, he saw peripherally that Ro Laren and Kasidy had just arrived, and that Quark was practically running to greet them.

Ezri grinned up at him. "I'll have you know that you're looking at *the* unofficial assistant commander for the *Defiant*'s first trip into the Gamma Quadrant."

"Ezri, that's wonderful," he said, meaning it. "And you're sure this is what you want . . ."

"Positive," she said. "And Vaughn's going to include his recommendation along with Kira's, that I'm put on a command track."

Julian touched the rim of her glass with his, feeling a sudden wave of warmth and love for her. They'd had several long talks since he'd woken up from surgery, about needs and expectations. Ezri's sudden decision to transfer to Command was something of a surprise, but she said that she was ready to commit herself . . . one of the immediate results being that she wouldn't need *quite* so much space to figure out what she wanted to do.

"I just finally realized that with as much potential as I have, I could stand around for years contemplating my choices," she said, lying in his arms, her ever-cold hands in his. "I want to get on with it, that's all. I'm ready."

Julian had surprised himself by trying to talk her out of it, afraid that she was only reacting to his near-death experience, but she insisted that while her fear had played a part in her resolution, it wasn't the only reason.

"You're worrying again," she said. "Quit it, Julian. I made up my mind, and I'm happy with my decision."

"Yes, but I don't want you to feel like—"

"—I don't," she said firmly. "And it might do you some good to remember that as much as I love you, you're probably going to be calling me 'sir' before too long."

Julian lowered his voice, leaning in. "I can call you sir now, if you like."

Her eyes sparkled as she looked over the rim of her glass. "Ask me again later," she said.

Julian promised her that he would.

Vaughn was enjoying himself thoroughly, talking and watching and relaxing. Kira was in a fine mood—and no wonder, she'd told him all about the prophecy situation and its outcome earlier—and though he'd already been impressed by her command in crisis, seeing her at ease and happy cinched his feelings. He was going to like working for her.

So far, he'd liked everyone he'd talked with. Vaughn had met most of the senior staff yesterday, and thought them a good mix. The only one he hadn't met formally was Ro Laren, and when he saw her talking to the Ferengi bartender, he started edging in her direction. Taran'atar, a little baffled but still game, was listening intently to Lieutenant Bowers recommending sociology texts he should look into.

Quark was smiling up at Ro with the unmistakable demeanor of the hopelessly smitten, shooting an unhappy glance in Vaughn's direction when he approached them.

"Nice party, Quark," Vaughn said. "Though I should probably tell you, that fruit wine of yours is right on the edge of going bad."

"I'll have to look into that," Quark said blankly, then smiled at Ro again. Vaughn noticed an odd smell coming from him.

"So, tomorrow night it is," Quark said, and Ro nodded. With another sullen look at Vaughn, the Ferengi hurried away, a definite spring in his step, taking his odor with him.

"Lieutenant Ro, I'm Elias Vaughn," he introduced himself, extending his hand. Ro shook a little hesitantly, but her grip was firm.

"Commander," she said, only meeting his eyes for an instant before looking away. He wasn't surprised; her disastrous reputation in Starfleet preceded her, and he knew from her files that she was something of an introvert.

"I hear you were top of your class at Advanced Tactical," Vaughn said. "You know, I helped design part of their curriculum. I'd be interested in hearing what you thought of the entire training experience; we should get together some time."

Ro nodded, her surprise showing in the slight widening of her eyes. "Sure. That would be fine. I'm sorry, Commander, if you'll excuse me . . ."

"Of course. Nice meeting you."

Ro quickly walked over to where Shar and Nog were, both young men greeting her warmly. Interesting; Vaughn looked forward to knowing her better. She'd led a life of extremes, and he found that while real adversity destroyed many, it also sculpted its survivors into some of the most intriguing personalities he'd ever known.

He wondered if she had any idea what Picard had done, after word had started to spread that she'd resurfaced on Bajor. Starfleet had been ready to clap her in irons and put her away for good, Bajoran government or no Bajoran government. But something about this woman had affected Jean-Luc profoundly, despite her betrayal. He'd actually lobbied Command behind the scenes on her behalf, quietly but insistently, until they agreed to let the Ro Laren matter drop. Starfleet might never go so far as to issue her a formal pardon, but because of Jean-Luc Picard, they would let her be.

Vaughn noticed that Taran'atar was starting to look a touch uncertain as he sniffed the air around Quark and went to rescue him, as happy as he'd been in years.

Ensign Prynn Tenmei ran her fingers through her short black hair and checked one more time to make sure her combadge was on straight as she strode toward the hall. She'd been so busy dealing with the *Defiant,* then the evacuation and its aftermath, that she'd only learned about the new XO and the welcoming reception an hour ago. One shower and fresh uniform later, she felt ready to meet her new commander, and she was determined to make a good first impression.

Tenmei took a deep breath, then another, stepped through the doors . . . and refused to believe what she saw.

Vaughn.

Oh, God. He's *the new first officer?*

He stood there, talking to Lieutenant Ro with a slight smile on his face.

Shaking with rage, Prynn turned before she could be noticed and bolted out the door. She walked quickly away, headed for her quarters. After a few seconds, she broke into a run.

Nerys had gone out of her way to invite Kasidy to the welcoming party. Kas had debated not going, but finally decided that she would stop by at least long enough to announce her decision, maybe longer depending on how she felt. She ran into Ro just outside the meeting hall, and the two women walked in together in a companionable silence. Kas liked Ro; she thought Bajor could use a few more like her.

Ro was immediately all but tackled by Quark, and looking around, Kasidy realized that she didn't want to stay; she wasn't in the mood for light conversation or company, although she had to admit that seeing Taran'atar for the first time definitely captured her attention. It wasn't every day that one saw a Jem'Hadar at a cocktail party.

Kira was talking to Ezri about something, but when she spotted Kas, she quickly extricated herself and hurried over, smiling a little anxiously.

"Kas, I'm so glad you decided to come."

Kasidy smiled, looking into her concerned, searching gaze and seeing how much Kira still wanted their friendship. She was glad for it, but also knew it wasn't ever going to be the same.

"Actually, I'm not staying," Kasidy said. "I'm feeling a little tired . . . but I wanted you to know that I've decided to go ahead with my plans to move to Bajor."

Relief flooded Kira's face. "That's wonderful. I just know it's the right thing for you, Kas, after all you've done with the house, and . . . and how much you've wanted it."

Kas patted the noticeable swell of her belly, thinking of Ben, thinking that there was just too much tying her to Bajor now. Wondering what her child's life would be.

"You're right," she said, softly. "It's what I want."

* * *

Only moments after Kasidy left, Kira got a call from ops; a personal line from Bajor was waiting in her office. Vaughn was in the middle of telling a pretty funny anecdote about having to take the Academy flight test with his very first hangover, but Kira didn't like leaving people on hold; she quietly excused herself from the small audience and slipped out of the meeting hall, hurrying across the Promenade to a turbolift.

On another day, she might have been annoyed at having to leave in the middle of such a pleasant gathering, but she was just too happy. Commander Vaughn was going to make an exceptional first officer; he was emotionally balanced, bright, experienced—and his brush with the Prophets made him the perfect choice for a Bajoran station.

An Orb is home, Bajor is opening up to new ideas, I have a great staff and great friends . . . and the station is safe.

Kas's plans to leave the sector had been the only thing that had still felt unresolved, and though Kira had hoped that the revelation of B'hala's secret crypts would change her mind, she hadn't been certain. Now, she felt a sense of completion, of things coming full circle—from her early-morning dream of a dying freighter and Benjamin to here and now, riding the lift to ops and knowing that she had a party of new and old friends to return to, she felt like she'd grown. She felt like for the first time in a while, there was nothing dark hiding in her life, waiting to surprise her.

She stepped into ops, nodding and smiling at the evening shift as she walked to her office. Not everything was perfect, of course—but happiness wasn't about achieving perfection. For her, happiness was about hope and feeling loved, about being competent at her job and in touch with herself, with her faith.

Life was good, maybe as good as it got.

20

Ro saw Kira leave, and found herself talking to Shar with one eye on the door, waiting for the colonel's return. After about ten minutes, she decided it might actually be better if she could have a few minutes with Kira in private. Besides, Quark was starting to circle again, and he smelled like he'd taken a shower in lightly rancid fuel oil.

Ezri said that Kira had been called to her office, so Ro slipped out of the party and headed for a turbolift. When the doors opened into ops, she saw that Kira was sitting at her desk, alone.

As Ro walked closer, she realized that Kira was working, a stack of reports in front of her and one in hand. She didn't want to interrupt the colonel, but Kira didn't know that she'd already filed her investigation report, and Ro wanted to make sure that Kira was ready for any fallout.

When the office doors slid open, Ro knocked on

the doorframe and Kira looked up, obviously preoccupied.

"Colonel, I'm sorry to bother you . . ."

"That's all right, come in," Kira said, setting the padd aside.

"I just wanted you to know that I sent my report on Istani's murder to the Ministry of Justice," Ro said, the doors closing behind her. "I included everything, but I kind of figure that with the killer dead, no one is going to want to look too hard at the Assembly's involvement. Anyway, I thought you should know, they may have some questions before they close the file."

"Thank you," Kira said. "Listen . . . I meant to tell you before that you did an exemplary job with the evacuation. With the investigation, too. Really outstanding work."

"I—thank you," Ro said, flustered and pleased. Kira had never said anything as nice to her, and it felt amazingly good, touching off a flush of warm pride.

"I was too quick to judge you, Ro, and I hope you'll accept my apology."

Ro hadn't planned on saying anything, but Kira's praise had caught her off guard, surprising her into it.

"Colonel, I should apologize, too. Being too quick to judge runs both ways, and I haven't made it easy for you."

Kira smiled slightly, but seemed to be looking past Ro, her thoughts elsewhere. There was something different about her, something . . .

"Maybe there comes a point when we all need to

start again," she said, brushing her hair behind her ears.

"Colonel, your earring," Ro said, immediately scanning the floor in front of Kira's desk. The clasp must have broken; she'd never seen Kira without it.

"I took it off," Kira said, still wearing that little smile, but Ro saw a profound sadness in her eyes. "It seems that Vedek Yevir got the last word, after all. I've been Attainted."

Ro stared at her. "You mean . . ."

"I mean that I am no longer welcome within the Bajoran faith," Kira said calmly. "I'm forbidden from entering any temple, nor can I study any of our prophecies, or wear my earring, or look into an Orb, or even pray with other Bajorans. Ever."

Kira's voice caught just a little on the last word, and she quickly swallowed it down, not sure why she'd told Ro, of all people, Yevir's calm and self-righteous expression still clear in her mind, his voice repeating over and over again.

"When you chose to go against the word of a vedek, you turned away from Their light, Nerys. I had no choice but to make the recommendation, and the Assembly agreed . . ."

She saw the open compassion and pity on Ro's face, saw that Ro was about to tell her how very sorry she was, and Kira suddenly realized that she couldn't bear it. That the words would kill her.

"Ro, I have work to do."

Ro nodded, seeming to understand, and that was awful, too. Without saying anything else, she turned and left the office. Kira picked up the report she'd been reading and found where she'd left off, concentrating, refusing to be beaten by one petty man, refusing to think of what he'd taken from her.

She still had her work; it would have to be enough.

EPILOGUE

It had been long enough; nothing was going to happen. It was time to go back.

Jake sat at the shuttle's controls, his shoulders slumped, a few empty ration packets cluttering the console. The flight plan was up on the screen, all set to retrace his path back to the station, and he couldn't help thinking that it looked a lot like failure. Nearly three full days, and all he had to show for it was a pinched nerve in his neck, from falling asleep in the pilot's seat on the second night. He hadn't brought a med kit, and all the *Venture* had on board was a few bandages and a half-empty tube of medicated foot lotion.

Jake massaged the sore muscles, scowling, focusing on the ache because he didn't particularly want to keep thinking about his grandiose washout. He'd already decided that when he returned to the station, he would tell his friends what he'd done. He didn't care anymore about being embarrassed. Dad was still gone and he'd let his own wild hope talk him into a big, stupid fantasy. He'd lied to people he cared about, but he could fix it . . . and maybe by talking to Ezri and Nog, to Kas, he'd be better able to come to terms with how he was feeling about his father.

And not just the good stuff, either. Jake loved and missed him terribly, but there was also a little anger, and some hurt. Dad was off having this incredible, enlightening experience, because it was his destiny . . . but whatever he was to the Prophets, he was also Jake's dad, and that relationship mattered. Yes, Jake was old enough to be on his own, but did that mean he was just supposed to let his father go with a smile and a wave?

Maybe so, Jake thought, and for the first time since Dad had gone, the thought wasn't a bitter one. Now that he was about to leave, about to let the prophecy go, he realized that his trip to the wormhole had brought him closer to an acceptance of the situation than all those weeks at B'hala. Maybe part of the reason he'd struggled so hard to avoid dealing with it was because he didn't want to feel angry or hurt . . . and he didn't want to accept that his father had willingly left him behind.

And that's okay. I don't have to be perfect . . . and neither does he.

He was disappointed that the prophecy hadn't come true, no question, and he wasn't looking forward to confessing his bizarre mission—but he *was* looking forward to going home. Maybe he would start another book, or look into the Pennington

School again, after Kas had the baby. Maybe he could do a lot of things, and when Dad *did* return to linear space, he'd be proud that Jake had gotten on with his life.

Jake straightened in his chair, feeling okay, feeling hopeful and a little bit excited about all of the possibilities in front of him. Not great, but not so bad, either. Maybe he'd misunderstood the prophecy, or it had never been real, or it wasn't even meant for him. Whatever it was, he suddenly felt like he hadn't wasted the last three days, after all.

"Going home," he said, tapping at the controls, telling the *Venture* to return him to the station. The shuttle had drifted some, but he'd be back at DS9 within the hour.

Jake hit the command key—and the shuttle spun around suddenly, the sensors reading a massive flush of energy surrounding him. They'd been out of whack for his entire trip, but he hadn't seen anything like this.

"Onscreen bow," he said, hearing the quaver of sudden hope in his voice, trying not to read too much into it—

—and what he saw on the screen made him laugh out loud, a pure sound of delight and wonder.

It's true, it's all true!

Swirling, dancing colors filled the screen, red and blue, white and purple, every color he'd ever seen in a kind of flowering mist. It was all around the *Venture,* streams of light flowing past the tiny ship in ribbons and waves. He could feel the power and the presence of consciousness, of an awareness, and his surprise was surpassed only by his joy; he might have been ready to let it all go, but it wasn't necessary anymore, the Prophets had come and he would see his father again, he'd be able to bring him home—

—except the colors were moving faster now, and the sensors told him that the shuttle was going too fast, that it was starting to spin as it was carried deeper into the wormhole.

A second later the artificial gravity went, and Jake grabbed for the straps of his chair, not laughing anymore. The ship was going even faster, he was getting dizzy and an alarm started to flash and beep, then another, then a third. His stomach lurching, Jake stabbed at the controls—and there was no response.

"Stop! Stop it!" Jake shouted, an empty ration pack flying in front of his face, the colors in front of him getting brighter, becoming blinding. The *Venture* couldn't take much more, it was going to tear apart, and his head was spinning along with the colors, they were blazing but things were getting darker, he was sick and he felt like he couldn't breathe—

The shuttle started to shake violently and all of the alarms died at once when the power cut out.

Just before Jake lost consciousness, he saw his father's unsmiling face in his mind's eye, he saw his father reaching out to touch him, and he thought that he might be dreaming, after all.

THE BEGINNING

ABOUT THE AUTHOR

S. D. (Stephani Danelle) Perry writes multimedia novelizations in the fantasy/science-fiction/horror realm for love and money. A two-time contributor to the acclaimed short story anthology *Star Trek: The Lives of Dax*, her other works include the bestselling *Resident Evil* series of novels, several *Aliens* novels, as well as the novelizations of *Timecop* and *Virus*. Under the name Stella Howard, she's written an original novel based upon the television series *Xena, Warrior Princess*. She lives in Portland, Oregon, with her husband and beloved dogs.

Look for STAR TREK fiction from Pocket Books

Star Trek®: The Original Series

Enterprise: The First Adventure • Vonda N. McIntyre
Final Frontier • Diane Carey
Strangers From the Sky • Margaret Wander Bonanno
Spock's World • Diane Duane
The Lost Years • J.M. Dillard
Probe • Margaret Wander Bonanno
Prime Directive • Judith and Garfield Reeves-Stevens
Best Destiny • Diane Carey
Shadows on the Sun • Michael Jan Friedman
Sarek • A.C. Crispin
Federation • Judith and Garfield Reeves-Stevens
Vulcan's Forge • Josepha Sherman & Susan Shwartz
Mission to Horatius • Mack Reynolds
Vulcan's Heart • Josepha Sherman & Susan Shwartz

Novelizations

Star Trek: The Motion Picture • Gene Roddenberry
Star Trek II: The Wrath of Khan • Vonda N. McIntyre
Star Trek III: The Search for Spock • Vonda N. McIntyre
Star Trek IV: The Voyage Home • Vonda N. McIntyre
Star Trek V: The Final Frontier • J.M. Dillard
Star Trek VI: The Undiscovered Country • J.M. Dillard
Star Trek Generations • J.M. Dillard
Starfleet Academy • Diane Carey

Star Trek books by William Shatner with Judith and Garfield Reeves-Stevens

The Ashes of Eden
The Return
Avenger
Star Trek: Odyssey (contains *The Ashes of Eden*, *The Return*, and *Avenger)*
Spectre
Dark Victory
Preserver

#1 • *Star Trek: The Motion Picture* • Gene Roddenberry
#2 • *The Entropy Effect* • Vonda N. McIntyre
#3 • *The Klingon Gambit* • Robert E. Vardeman
#4 • *The Covenant of the Crown* • Howard Weinstein
#5 • *The Prometheus Design* • Sondra Marshak & Myrna Culbreath

#6 • *The Abode of Life* • Lee Correy
#7 • *Star Trek II: The Wrath of Khan* • Vonda N. McIntyre
#8 • *Black Fire* • Sonni Cooper
#9 • *Triangle* • Sondra Marshak & Myrna Culbreath
#10 • *Web of the Romulans* • M.S. Murdock
#11 • *Yesterday's Son* • A.C. Crispin
#12 • *Mutiny on the Enterprise* • Robert E. Vardeman
#13 • *The Wounded Sky* • Diane Duane
#14 • *The Trellisane Confrontation* • David Dvorkin
#15 • *Corona* • Greg Bear
#16 • *The Final Reflection* • John M. Ford
#17 • *Star Trek III: The Search for Spock* • Vonda N. McIntyre
#18 • *My Enemy, My Ally* • Diane Duane
#19 • *The Tears of the Singers* • Melinda Snodgrass
#20 • *The Vulcan Academy Murders* • Jean Lorrah
#21 • *Uhura's Song* • Janet Kagan
#22 • *Shadow Lord* • Laurence Yep
#23 • *Ishmael* • Barbara Hambly
#24 • *Killing Time* • Della Van Hise
#25 • *Dwellers in the Crucible* • Margaret Wander Bonanno
#26 • *Pawns and Symbols* • Majliss Larson
#27 • *Mindshadow* • J.M. Dillard
#28 • *Crisis on Centaurus* • Brad Ferguson
#29 • *Dreadnought!* • Diane Carey
#30 • *Demons* • J.M. Dillard
#31 • *Battlestations!* • Diane Carey
#32 • *Chain of Attack* • Gene DeWeese
#33 • *Deep Domain* • Howard Weinstein
#34 • *Dreams of the Raven* • Carmen Carter
#35 • *The Romulan Way* • Diane Duane & Peter Morwood
#36 • *How Much for Just the Planet?* • John M. Ford
#37 • *Bloodthirst* • J.M. Dillard
#38 • *The IDIC Epidemic* • Jean Lorrah
#39 • *Time for Yesterday* • A.C. Crispin
#40 • *Timetrap* • David Dvorkin
#41 • *The Three-Minute Universe* • Barbara Paul
#42 • *Memory Prime* • Judith and Garfield Reeves-Stevens
#43 • *The Final Nexus* • Gene DeWeese
#44 • *Vulcan's Glory* • D.C. Fontana
#45 • *Double, Double* • Michael Jan Friedman
#46 • *The Cry of the Onlies* • Judy Klass
#47 • *The Kobayashi Maru* • Julia Ecklar
#48 • *Rules of Engagement* • Peter Morwood

#49 • *The Pandora Principle* • Carolyn Clowes
#50 • *Doctor's Orders* • Diane Duane
#51 • *Unseen Enemy* • V.E. Mitchell
#52 • *Home Is the Hunter* • Dana Kramer Rolls
#53 • *Ghost-Walker* • Barbara Hambly
#54 • *A Flag Full of Stars* • Brad Ferguson
#55 • *Renegade* • Gene DeWeese
#56 • *Legacy* • Michael Jan Friedman
#57 • *The Rift* • Peter David
#58 • *Face of Fire* • Michael Jan Friedman
#59 • *The Disinherited* • Peter David
#60 • *Ice Trap* • L.A. Graf
#61 • *Sanctuary* • John Vornholt
#62 • *Death Count* • L.A. Graf
#63 • *Shell Game* • Melissa Crandall
#64 • *The Starship Trap* • Mel Gilden
#65 • *Windows on a Lost World* • V.E. Mitchell
#66 • *From the Depths* • Victor Milan
#67 • *The Great Starship Race* • Diane Carey
#68 • *Firestorm* • L.A. Graf
#69 • *The Patrian Transgression* • Simon Hawke
#70 • *Traitor Winds* • L.A. Graf
#71 • *Crossroad* • Barbara Hambly
#72 • *The Better Man* • Howard Weinstein
#73 • *Recovery* • J.M. Dillard
#74 • *The Fearful Summons* • Denny Martin Flynn
#75 • *First Frontier* • Diane Carey & Dr. James I. Kirkland
#76 • *The Captain's Daughter* • Peter David
#77 • *Twilight's End* • Jerry Oltion
#78 • *The Rings of Tautee* • Dean Wesley Smith & Kristine Kathryn Rusch
#79 • *Invasion!* #1: *First Strike* • Diane Carey
#80 • *The Joy Machine* • James Gunn
#81 • *Mudd in Your Eye* • Jerry Oltion
#82 • *Mind Meld* • John Vornholt
#83 • *Heart of the Sun* • Pamela Sargent & George Zebrowski
#84 • *Assignment: Eternity* • Greg Cox
#85-87 • *My Brother's Keeper* • Michael Jan Friedman
  #85 • *Republic*
  #86 • *Constitution*
  #87 • *Enterprise*
#88 • *Across the Universe* • Pamela Sargent & George Zebrowski
#89-94 • *New Earth*

#89 • *Wagon Train to the Stars* • Diane Carey
#90 • *Belle Terre* • Dean Wesley Smith with Diane Carey
#91 • *Rough Trails* • L.A. Graf
#92 • *The Flaming Arrow* • Kathy and Jerry Oltion
#93 • *Thin Air* • Kristine Kathryn Rusch & Dean Wesley Smith
#94 • *Challenger* • Diane Carey
#95-96 • *Rihannsu* • Diane Duane
#95 • *Swordhunt*
#96 • *The Empty Throne*

Star Trek: The Next Generation®

Metamorphosis • Jean Lorrah
Vendetta • Peter David
Reunion • Michael Jan Friedman
Imzadi • Peter David
The Devil's Heart • Carmen Carter
Dark Mirror • Diane Duane
Q-Squared • Peter David
Crossover • Michael Jan Friedman
Kahless • Michael Jan Friedman
Ship of the Line • Diane Carey
The Best and the Brightest • Susan Wright
Planet X • Michael Jan Friedman
Imzadi II: Triangle • Peter David
I, Q • Peter David & John de Lancie
The Valiant • Michael Jan Friedman
The Genesis Wave, Book One • John Vornholt
The Genesis Wave, Book Two • John Vornholt

Novelizations
Encounter at Farpoint • David Gerrold
Unification • Jeri Taylor
Relics • Michael Jan Friedman
Descent • Diane Carey
All Good Things... • Michael Jan Friedman
Star Trek: Klingon • Dean Wesley Smith & Kristine Kathryn Rusch
Star Trek Generations • J.M. Dillard
Star Trek: First Contact • J.M. Dillard
Star Trek: Insurrection • J.M. Dillard

#1 • *Ghost Ship* • Diane Carey
#2 • *The Peacekeepers* • Gene DeWeese
#3 • *The Children of Hamlin* • Carmen Carter
#4 • *Survivors* • Jean Lorrah

#5 • *Strike Zone* • Peter David
#6 • *Power Hungry* • Howard Weinstein
#7 • *Masks* • John Vornholt
#8 • *The Captain's Honor* • David & Daniel Dvorkin
#9 • *A Call to Darkness* • Michael Jan Friedman
#10 • *A Rock and a Hard Place* • Peter David
#11 • *Gulliver's Fugitives* • Keith Sharee
#12 • *Doomsday World* • David, Carter, Friedman & Greenberger
#13 • *The Eyes of the Beholders* • A.C. Crispin
#14 • *Exiles* • Howard Weinstein
#15 • *Fortune's Light* • Michael Jan Friedman
#16 • *Contamination* • John Vornholt
#17 • *Boogeymen* • Mel Gilden
#18 • *Q-in-Law* • Peter David
#19 • *Perchance to Dream* • Howard Weinstein
#20 • *Spartacus* • T.L. Mancour
#21 • *Chains of Command* • W.A. McCoy & E.L. Flood
#22 • *Imbalance* • V.E. Mitchell
#23 • *War Drums* • John Vornholt
#24 • *Nightshade* • Laurell K. Hamilton
#25 • *Grounded* • David Bischoff
#26 • *The Romulan Prize* • Simon Hawke
#27 • *Guises of the Mind* • Rebecca Neason
#28 • *Here There Be Dragons* • John Peel
#29 • *Sins of Commission* • Susan Wright
#30 • *Debtor's Planet* • W.R. Thompson
#31 • *Foreign Foes* • Dave Galanter & Greg Brodeur
#32 • *Requiem* • Michael Jan Friedman & Kevin Ryan
#33 • *Balance of Power* • Dafydd ab Hugh
#34 • *Blaze of Glory* • Simon Hawke
#35 • *The Romulan Stratagem* • Robert Greenberger
#36 • *Into the Nebula* • Gene DeWeese
#37 • *The Last Stand* • Brad Ferguson
#38 • *Dragon's Honor* • Kij Johnson & Greg Cox
#39 • *Rogue Saucer* • John Vornholt
#40 • *Possession* • J.M. Dillard & Kathleen O'Malley
#41 • *Invasion! #2: The Soldiers of Fear* • Dean Wesley Smith & Kristine Kathryn Rusch
#42 • *Infiltrator* • W.R. Thompson
#43 • *A Fury Scorned* • Pamela Sargent & George Zebrowski
#44 • *The Death of Princes* • John Peel
#45 • *Intellivore* • Diane Duane
#46 • *To Storm Heaven* • Esther Friesner
#47-49 • *The Q Continuum* • Greg Cox

#47 • *Q-Space*
#48 • *Q-Zone*
#49 • *Q-Strike*
#50 • *Dyson Sphere* • Charles Pellegrino & George Zebrowski
#51-56 • *Double Helix*
#51 • *Infection* • John Gregory Betancourt
#52 • *Vectors* • Dean Wesley Smith & Kristine Kathryn Rusch
#53 • *Red Sector* • Diane Carey
#54 • *Quarantine* • John Vornholt
#55 • *Double or Nothing* • Peter David
#56 • *The First Virtue* • Michael Jan Friedman & Christie Golden
#57 • *The Forgotten War* • William Forstchen
#58-59 • *Gemworld* • John Vornholt
#58 • *Gemworld #1*
#59 • *Gemworld #2*
#60 • *Tooth and Claw* • Doranna Durgin
#61 • *Diplomatic Implausibility* • Keith R.A. DeCandido
#62-63 • *Maximum Warp* • Dave Galanter & Greg Brodeur
#62 • *Maximum Warp* #1
#63 • *Maximum Warp* #2

Star Trek: Deep Space Nine®

Warped • K.W. Jeter
Legends of the Ferengi • Ira Steven Behr & Robert Hewitt Wolfe
The Lives of Dax • Marco Palmieri, ed.
Millennium • Judith and Garfield Reeves-Stevens
#1 • *The Fall of Terok Nor*
#2 • *The War of the Prophets*
#3 • *Inferno*
Novelizations
Emissary • J.M. Dillard
The Search • Diane Carey
The Way of the Warrior • Diane Carey
Star Trek: Klingon • Dean Wesley Smith & Kristine Kathryn Rusch
Trials and Tribble-ations • Diane Carey
Far Beyond the Stars • Steve Barnes
What You Leave Behind • Diane Carey

#1 • *Emissary* • J.M. Dillard
#2 • *The Siege* • Peter David
#3 • *Bloodletter* • K.W. Jeter

#4 • *The Big Game* • Sandy Schofield
#5 • *Fallen Heroes* • Dafydd ab Hugh
#6 • *Betrayal* • Lois Tilton
#7 • *Warchild* • Esther Friesner
#8 • *Antimatter* • John Vornholt
#9 • *Proud Helios* • Melissa Scott
#10 • *Valhalla* • Nathan Archer
#11 • *Devil in the Sky* • Greg Cox & John Gregory Betancourt
#12 • *The Laertian Gamble* • Robert Sheckley
#13 • *Station Rage* • Diane Carey
#14 • *The Long Night* • Dean Wesley Smith & Kristine Kathryn Rusch
#15 • *Objective: Bajor* • John Peel
#16 • *Invasion! #3: Time's Enemy* • L.A. Graf
#17 • *The Heart of the Warrior* • John Gregory Betancourt
#18 • *Saratoga* • Michael Jan Friedman
#19 • *The Tempest* • Susan Wright
#20 • *Wrath of the Prophets* • David, Friedman & Greenberger
#21 • *Trial by Error* • Mark Garland
#22 • *Vengeance* • Dafydd ab Hugh
#23 • *The 34th Rule* • Armin Shimerman & David R. George III
#24-26 • *Rebels* • Dafydd ab Hugh
  #24 • *The Conquered*
  #25 • *The Courageous*
  #26 • *The Liberated*
#27 • *A Stitch in Time* • Andrew J. Robinson
Avatar • S.D. Perry
  #1 • S.D. Perry
  #2 • S.D. Perry

Star Trek: Voyager®

Mosaic • Jeri Taylor
Pathways • Jeri Taylor
Captain Proton: Defender of the Earth • D.W. "Prof" Smith
Novelizations
  Caretaker • L.A. Graf
  Flashback • Diane Carey
  Day of Honor • Michael Jan Friedman
  Equinox • Diane Carey

#1 • *Caretaker* • L.A. Graf
#2 • *The Escape* • Dean Wesley Smith & Kristine Kathryn Rusch

#3 • *Ragnarok* • Nathan Archer
#4 • *Violations* • Susan Wright
#5 • *Incident at Arbuk* • John Gregory Betancourt
#6 • *The Murdered Sun* • Christie Golden
#7 • *Ghost of a Chance* • Mark A. Garland & Charles G. McGraw
#8 • *Cybersong* • S.N. Lewitt
#9 • *Invasion! #4: Final Fury* • Dafydd ab Hugh
#10 • *Bless the Beasts* • Karen Haber
#11 • *The Garden* • Melissa Scott
#12 • *Chrysalis* • David Niall Wilson
#13 • *The Black Shore* • Greg Cox
#14 • *Marooned* • Christie Golden
#15 • *Echoes* • Dean Wesley Smith, Kristine Kathryn Rusch & Nina Kiriki Hoffman
#16 • *Seven of Nine* • Christie Golden
#17 • *Death of a Neutron Star* • Eric Kotani
#18 • *Battle Lines* • Dave Galanter & Greg Brodeur
#19-21 • *Dark Matters* • Christie Golden
 #19 • *Cloak and Dagger*
 #20 • *Ghost Dance*
 #21 • *Shadow of Heaven*

Star Trek®: New Frontier

New Frontier #1-4 Collector's Edition • Peter David
 #1 •*House of Cards*
 #2 •*Into the Void*
 #3 •*The Two-Front War*
 #4 •*End Game*
#5 • *Martyr* • Peter David
#6 • *Fire on High* • Peter David
The Captain's Table #5 • *Once Burned* • Peter David
Double Helix #5 • *Double or Nothing* • Peter David
#7 • *The Quiet Place* • Peter David
#8 • *Dark Allies* • Peter David
#9-11 • *Excalibur* • Peter David
 #9 • *Requiem*
 #10 • *Renaissance*
 #11 • *Restoration*

Star Trek®: Invasion!

#1 • *First Strike* • Diane Carey
#2 • *The Soldiers of Fear* • Dean Wesley Smith & Kristine Kathryn Rusch
#3 • *Time's Enemy* • L.A. Graf
#4 • *Final Fury* • Dafydd ab Hugh
Invasion! Omnibus • various

Star Trek®: Day of Honor

#1 • *Ancient Blood* • Diane Carey
#2 • *Armageddon Sky* • L.A. Graf
#3 • *Her Klingon Soul* • Michael Jan Friedman
#4 • *Treaty's Law* • Dean Wesley Smith & Kristine Kathryn Rusch
The Television Episode • Michael Jan Friedman
Day of Honor Omnibus • various

Star Trek®: The Captain's Table

#1 • *War Dragons* • L.A. Graf
#2 • *Dujonian's Hoard* • Michael Jan Friedman
#3 • *The Mist* • Dean Wesley Smith & Kristine Kathryn Rusch
#4 • *Fire Ship* • Diane Carey
#5 • *Once Burned* • Peter David
#6 • *Where Sea Meets Sky* • Jerry Oltion
The Captain's Table Omnibus • various

Star Trek®: The Dominion War

#1 • *Behind Enemy Lines* • John Vornholt
#2 • *Call to Arms...* • Diane Carey
#3 • *Tunnel Through the Stars* • John Vornholt
#4 • *...Sacrifice of Angels* • Diane Carey

Star Trek®: The Badlands

#1 • Susan Wright
#2 • Susan Wright

Star Trek®: Dark Passions

#1 • Susan Wright
#2 • Susan Wright

Other Books

Legends of the Ferengi • Ira Steven Behr & Robert Hewitt Wolfe
Strange New Worlds, vols. I, II, and III • Dean Wesley Smith, ed.
Adventures in Time and Space • Mary P. Taylor
Captain Proton: Defender of the Earth • D.W. "Prof" Smith
New Worlds, New Civilizations • Michael Jan Friedman
The Lives of Dax • Marco Palmieri, ed.
The Klingon Hamlet • Wil'yam Shex'pir
Enterprise Logs • Carol Greenburg, ed.